# You Complicate Me

## Alicia Wag

**ForbiddenFiction**
www.forbiddenfiction.com

an imprint of

**Fantastic Fiction Publishing**
www.fantasticfictionpublishing.com

YOU COMPLICATE ME
A Forbidden Fiction book

Fantastic Fiction Publishing
Hayward, California

© Alicia Wag, 2016

**CREDITS**
Editor: Lon Sarver, Derrick N. Davidson
Cover Design: Siolnatine
Cover photos: Dundanim and Maxsaf at Dreamstime
Production Editor: Kaye O'Malley
Proofreading: Kailin Morgan


SKU: AW1-000276-02 FFP
ISBN: 978-1-62234-302-7

Published in the United States of America

# I was about to put the last receipt

in the 'Q' folder when a man's voice said, "Hello, Annemarie." I froze. "Or should I call you Ms. Fitch?"

The receipt fell from my trembling fingers into the file cabinet. I coolly slid the drawer closed, turned, and smiled. "Annemarie is fine," I said. "Mr. Link."

He laughed, a sound like chimes ringing. "Call me Zach. Please."

I tried to ignore these pleasantries and get back to business. "Is there something I can help you with?"

"No," he shook his head. "My room is all set, thanks to you." I wasn't going to bother telling him it was Carol who dealt with the chair. He shot me that fantastic smile that lit up his whole face. It really was admirably put together. Square jaw, defined yet rugged cheekbones, strong nose, deep set and intense eyes, and full, shapely lips. And the head of wavy, black hair with the slightly messy look—wow. He was as handsome as Richard. More handsome, possibly. I shuddered at the thought and immediately blocked it out.

# Also recommended...

You may also enjoy these other ForbiddenFiction works:

### Deep Focus by M.L. Caufax
Zöe is nervous and excited to begin her first year at the exclusive university tucked away in a tiny forest town. Her new boss, Dean, is a handsome older man with captivating blue eyes, and an understanding smile. Everyone comes to him for counsel, even the townsfolk down the hill, because Dean always knows exactly what they should do. At Dean's suggestion, it seems only natural that Zöe should submit to her classmate Trevor's commanding advances when he comes to Dean for grief counseling after a bad breakup. Why shouldn't they put on erotic plays for Counselor Dean whenever he pleases? It no big deal - they'll only forget again when they leave, to focus on more important things like school work. Only when Zöe is gifted with an ancient talisman that protects her from Dean's hypnotic gaze does she finally discover the horrible truth... (M/F, M/F/M)
http://forbiddenfiction.com/story/mlc-1.000124/

### Held in Dreams by Ava Burquette
Elaine is an ordinary human with ordinary dreams, maybe a little too shy for her own good. At least that's what she tells herself, until she is kidnapped off of a city bus by a strange and charismatic man named Ghalib who has come looking specifically for her. Ghalib definitely isn't ordinary. He isn't even human. He's a Dream Architect, one of the beings who create dreams for humanity. His world is the realm of passion, imagination and nightmares, where humans may be kept as pets, or personal slaves. Ghalib is obsessed with Elaine, whose vivid, erotic dreams he finds irresistible. If Elaine is to contend with Ghalib on her own terms, she'll have to do more than let go of her shy, inhibited waking manner. She will have to realize her own dreams. (F/M. F/F, M/M)
http://forbiddenfiction.com/story/ab1-1-000093/

# DISCLAIMER

This book is a work of fiction which contains explicit erotic content; it is intended for mature readers. Do not read this if it's not legal for you.

All the characters, locations and events herein are fictional. While elements of existing locations or historical characters or events may be used fictitiously, any resemblance to actual people, places or events is coincidental.

This story is not intended to be used as an instruction manual. It may contain descriptions of erotic acts that are immoral, illegal, or unsafe. Do not take the events in this story as proof of the plausibility or safety of any particular practice.

To my friends; you know who you are.

# Contents

# Chapter 1
# Happily Ever After?

## ANNEMARIE

People say there's no such thing as a perfect life and that women can't have it all. I've made it my mission to prove them wrong. Of course I know that perfection is subjective, based on the desires, hopes, and dreams of the individual. My definitions were always the traditional ones—a good job, a gorgeous husband with a good job, a beautiful house, travel, friends, and eventually (very eventually, and maybe) a family.

My practicality put me right on track, but is life ever predictable? I thought so, once. Now, things are different. Lilah is still shaking her head, but I've learned not to be surprised by much of anything, even her.

That took me a while. I knew Lilah and I didn't have a lot in common, but I had no idea how different we were until she answered my ad on the hotel bulletin board and became my roommate. Don't get me wrong, she's my best friend and I love her dearly, but our lifestyles were polar opposites. I, for example, after man shopping for quite a while, had become laser focused on snagging Richard. Lilah was focused on anyone, man or woman, she could lure into bed. That might have been a problem, but fortunately, I have a white noise machine that spared me the sound effects.

I needled Lilah about her escapades, but they never really bothered me, nor did they interest me—much. Eventually that all changed, but the day we went shopping for Lilah's maid of honor dress, I was still in fantasy land.

"Do I have to wear pink?" she complained.

"It's not pink, it's champagne," I said. "And stop frowning, you'll get wrinkles." Lilah stood in front of the full length mirror, surveying herself.

The look on her face had gone from skeptical to pleased. "It's the one," I said, admiring the vintage lace and taffeta.

Lilah nodded absently, staring off into space. I peered beyond her image in the mirror and saw that it wasn't the cosmos she was staring at, it was the rear end of the sales associate, who was bending over to put away the strapless bras we hadn't ended up needing. If I had to use one word to describe Lilah's breasts, it would be perky.

The saleswoman stood and turned around to rejoin us. "How are we doing?" she asked as she approached, then nodded in approval when she saw Lilah. "That's gorgeous."

"We'll take it," I said.

"Are you sure?" said Lilah, looking skeptical again. "The pink might clash with your red hair."

"It's not pink," I said. "It's champagne, and it's the one."

"Are you going to make your sister wear one, too?"

My sister, who would refuse to wear a dress, was going to be a challenge. "No," I said. "But she's not the maid of honor, anyway, you are."

"Why do you always have to be so sure about everything?" asked Lilah, letting the saleswoman unzip her.

"Second guessing is for losers," I said. "I have to meet Richard; I'll see you at home." I had plenty of time, but I didn't need to be present while Lilah put on her flirt, and the extra minutes would allow me to forgo the bus and walk to the restaurant where Richard and I were having lunch. I'd been spending an hour a day at the hotel gym since the engagement, but with the arrival of spring and better weather, I vowed to increase my fitness by walking more.

When I got to the restaurant, I peered through the window and saw Richard already seated, looking studiously at his tablet. His sport coat hung neatly on the back of his chair as he leaned slightly forward, his horn-rimmed glasses perched on his regal nose, his full lips parted slightly in concentration. I imagined he was engaging in his lunchtime habit, reading The New York Times, and he looked so adorable doing it that I could hardly bear to interrupt.

The waiter did, though, showing up at the table with a glass of sparkling water for Richard and a steaming cup which I knew was filled with jasmine green tea, my current beverage of choice. I entered the warm restaurant and Richard saw me immediately, standing up and flashing his pearly whites. "Hey," he said, taking me in his arms and planting a big kiss on my lips.

"Hey yourself," I whispered. We were simply having lunch before Richard went back to work, but that didn't stop the clench between my legs, or the bulge I could feel growing in Richard's pants.

He let me go and I sat down, enjoying a sip of fragrant tea. "You're wearing my favorite tie," I said, noting the slim burgundy number I'd given him at the holidays.

"It's my favorite, too," he said, reaching across the table and taking my hand. I loved Richard's style and that even though there was no dress code at the software company where he worked, he never wore jeans or T-shirts to the office. Some of the other programmers teased him about it, but I knew that he was so much more than a strait-laced computer nerd.

The thought of that made my insides tingle again. "How hungry are you?" I asked.

"For food, you mean?" He smiled conspiratorially, and I knew we were on the same page.

"Do we have time?" I asked.

He answered by leaving a twenty dollar bill on the table and taking my hand. "Come on," he said.

We stayed glued to each other, Richard breathing into my ear and whispering naughty things while the valet got his car. From there, it was just a few minutes to my apartment. Thankfully and not surprisingly, Lilah wasn't back yet. I imagined she was trying to cement a rendezvous with the saleswoman.

The foreplay had already happened on the sidewalk and during the car ride, when I alternately licked Richard's ear and told him what I wanted him to do to me—politely, of course. We didn't have a lot of time, anyway, so I went straight to the bedroom and got naked.

Richard did the same, and in a minute we were tongue to tongue, skin to skin. "You feel so good, baby." Richard's eyes were closed, his head back, his dark hair curled into sweaty ringlets, relaxed, taking it slow, just the way I liked it. Nice and easy, position after position, controlled—until I said it was time. Then, and only then, could he let go and fuck me hard.

"Is it good?" Richard asked, looking into my eyes. I was on my back, Richard on his knees, his hands cradling my ass cheeks, lifting them off the bed.

"Yes," I answered. We both looked at Richard's sex sliding in and out. After several more easy thrusts, I whispered, "Now," and Richard pulled out.

I turned over and got onto my hands and knees so Richard could slip in from behind, probing me slow and deep. When I was ready, I said "Harder," and Richard sped up. While Richard rode me, I reached one hand between my legs and touched myself, feeling the delicious wave build up inside me. "I'm coming," I yelled, which was Richard's cue to join me.

I felt the throb of his sex follow my own orgasm like an echo, the way he always followed me, the way I liked it.

We cuddled together on the bed, and I thought again how lucky I was to have lassoed this man with the perfect, chiseled face and dreamy eyes. His body was pretty great, too. Who'd have thought a computer geek could be so buff? Rowing and hiking worked wonders for his taut physique, lurking underneath the suits and chinos.

He was like my own precious secret. My mastery over him filled a deep need, one I told no one about, not even Lilah.

The things we did were my dirty little secrets.

He was mine. All mine. Only mine.

## LILAH

I complained about the dress, but really I liked it. Lace wasn't my thing, but it was vintage, which was good, and like Annemarie said, it wasn't actually pink. Mostly, though, I didn't really care about the dress. I'd only be wearing it once, for a few hours on Annemarie's big day.

What was really awesome about the dress was Sharada. Annemarie left at exactly the right time, but she probably knew that. We'd gotten into pretty good sync since working at the hotel together and becoming room-mates. I'd known Annemarie a long time, since she became the youngest guest relations director at The Sentinel, and I became the youngest head pastry chef.

When Sharada unzipped me, and her hand lingered just a little too long at the small of my back, I knew she was feeling it, too. Thankfully, Annemarie was good and gone, so I turned around and dropped the dress, a gentle poof falling to the floor. There I stood in nothing but my black bikinis, nipples at attention. Sharada didn't bother with her hands, she just peered up at me questioningly with deep dark eyes rimmed with more charcoal pencil than I've ever used in my life. I nodded, and she dipped her head forward and tongued my nipples until my pussy was so wet I could feel my undies dampen.

We went into the fitting room together, and I tore through my bag fast for a dental dam. I pulled one out, watermelon flavor, just the thing for dreaming of summer and the warmer climes to come in a few months. Sharada had me on the bench, pantyless and spread-eagled, before I could count to ten, and I barely had enough time to plant the dental dam on me before she dove in.

Her lovely mouth turned out to be quite skilled, and I relaxed my butt into the hard fitting room bench and let her work my pussy while I played with my nipples. When I came, she looked up for a second and smiled, then went right back to work, which was fine with me. I would have felt gypped with only one orgasm.

It wasn't to be, though. After a few seconds, the bell on the shop door jingled, which I didn't think was any kind of a problem since Sharada wasn't the only employee in the store. It turned out to be, though. At the sound of a deep male voice, Sharada shot up, looking terrified. Eyes wide, she checked her face in the mirror, and saw with dismay that her red lipstick was smeared all over her chin. She grabbed a Kleenex and wiped it off as best she could, then disappeared.

I rummaged through my bag yet again and found my trusty travel-sized vibrator. In a few minutes, I'd finished the job Sharada had started, gotten dressed, and emerged. There she was, smiling and talking to a severe looking man. I spied the giant rock on her left hand and put two and two together.

She barely looked at me when I left, and I figured I wouldn't be seeing Sharada again, which was fine. I had no shortage of relationships in my life; I didn't need to add another to the mix.

Marriage. Why did people do it, anyway? Such a narrow, binding contract, full of unrealistic demands. If I ever married, it would likely be to more than one person, and we wouldn't make promises we couldn't keep, or have stupid rules to hold each other back.

Like Annemarie, for instance. She was brilliant, except when it came to Richard. She never talked about him beyond the superficial. His job, his hobbies, their wedding that was coming up at the end of summer. But I knew. I was a genius with men and their inner worlds. It came from knowing instinctively what turned them on. Annemarie turned Richard on, but there was a lot he hadn't tried. I could see it in the way he looked at me, and sometimes in the way he looked at Annemarie.

As far as she was concerned, Richard was everything she wanted. Problem was, the Richard she wanted was the one she chose to see. She'd always done that, and she'd always gotten hurt. Annemarie's gift was making people happy. She knew how to smooth things over when they were rough, and how to satisfy the pickiest guests. She knew how to please, but when it came to men, she inevitably bombed. She wanted to control things. It was understandable, given that she was so busy the rest of the time fixing things for everybody else, but it was no long term plan for a relationship.

My phone buzzed with a text from Jenn, asking whether I had time for tea. Jenn was my best employee in the kitchen, a great friend, and a woman of many talents. I knew exactly what tea time meant, and I definitely had time for it, especially after my somewhat unsatisfying encounter with Sharada.

It was a five minute bus ride to Jenn's, and when I arrived, she was wearing nothing but my favorite orange cock. I fell on my knees before it and took it in my mouth, sucking it, pulling and pushing it to stimulate Jenn's bare mound and clit. "That's it, baby," she moaned. "Just like that."

I stood, tore off my clothes and kissed Jenn hard, feeling our tits rub against each other and the cock tickle my pussy. "Get down," Jenn hissed, and I lay on the floor and opened my legs. I was so primed that the air on my clit felt stimulating, but it was nothing compared to Jenn's fingers gently brushing my swollen lips. "So ready," she said. I moaned affirmatively as she played with me lightly, teasingly. "You want me to fuck you?" I moaned again and Jenn said, "I can't hear you."

"Yes, baby," I said. "Fuck me, please."

"What was that?" Jenn whispered, shoving a finger into my hole. "What?"

"Fuck me," I said, louder, grabbing the back of Jenn's neck to pull her toward me. "Fuck me now."

I felt the orange cock fill me up, slowly. "Like this?" said Jenn, withdrawing the cock and slipping it in again, inch by inch. I settled back and closed my eyes, letting myself feel every moment of the cock moving in and out of me in excruciatingly blissful slow motion, grabbing a nip at Jenn's tits every time she lowered her body enough for them to be in proximity of my mouth.

She was feeling it, too, moaning along with me, and picking up speed. "Yes," I said as she moved faster. "Fuck me like that." The pounding was excruciatingly satisfying, but suddenly Jenn stopped and yelled for me to turn over.

I did, and she took me from behind, slapping my ass cheeks with every thrust, grabbing them and squeezing when she came. After collapsing on me for a second, she gently turned me over, slipped a finger inside me, and nursed my pussy with her mouth until I exploded.

We lay there together and snuggled for a few minutes, then got up and took a shower, and while Jenn made us hazelnut coffee with her Keurig, I told her about the dress and Sharada.

"Seriously?" she said. "I'm going to go in there and shop for a dress."

"It's a bridal shop," I said. "You're not getting married."

"Who cares," she said. "You think everyone who goes in there is getting married? I can pretend." I laughed. Jenn would probably do it. She was as game for adventure as I was. I'd never say it to Annemarie, but I could as easily have called Jenn my best friend, too. "You think Annemarie will really do it?" she asked.

"Do what?"

"Get married."

"Of course," I said. "Why wouldn't she?"

"I don't know," said Jenn, twirling a spoon in her coffee. "It seems like such a waste."

I laughed. "Now, Jenn," I said. "I know we both have a thing for her, but stop dreaming. She's as straight as they come."

"I don't know about that," said Jenn, shaking her adorable head. "I don't get that."

"Well, you're wrong," I said. "I would know."

# Chapter 2
# Summertime

**LILAH**

I love life. I love men, I love women, and I love sex. When it comes to the latter, I've never believed in limiting myself, and I credit much of my happiness to that fact. It's my opinion that most people, even those who live conventional, monogamous lives, would prefer to be like me. Richard, for example. He was obviously head over heels for Annemarie, and who wouldn't be? She was a tough nut, though, and insisted on controlling everything.

Richard played the game, and I know he liked being the bottom, but my hunch that there was more to him than met the eye proved true. He had deep down longings like the rest of us, and Annemarie just didn't want to see that. Richard was pretending right along with her, but wedding bells get a person going, and as the date drew nigh, the shit started to hit the fan.

When he broke down in our kitchen and told me he didn't know whether he could go through with it, I wasn't surprised. Annemarie had gotten held up at the hotel, and Richard was waiting for her. "Lilah," he said, his fingers raking the thick mop of ebony curls on his head. I pulled up a chair and took his hand in mine in a comforting kind of way. "Yeah, hon?"

His eyes were filled with fear and fire, making him look even sexier than usual. "I love Annemarie."

I massaged his hand, feeling the sinews and knuckles. "Of course you do."

"There's just—" He paused, looking straight at me, and for one fleeting second our hormones connected, and I felt a little tingle between my legs. Then he let it go. It wasn't the first time, after all. "There's stuff I have to figure out."

I heard footsteps on the stairs and dropped his hand. "Do what you need to do," I said. "I'll take care of her."

Annemarie came in, breathless and beautiful. The humid, late June heat did nothing to ruin her auburn locks, which looked good no matter what the weather. Her hair was in a French twist at the back, very professional, very classy. I especially liked peeking into her office at the hotel and seeing her with her reading glasses on, the ones that sat low on her nose, the way she peered over them with perfectly made up green eyes. Annemarie could see just fine. The glasses were part of the persona that made her so good at what she did. "Darling," she cried, hugging Richard. "What a day."

She fell into a kitchen chair, dropped her briefcase on the table and kicked off her black sandals. They left faint indentations on her pretty feet, feet I always thought would look great with henna tattoos on them, but no matter how many times I offered to adorn her with them, she turned me down. Her blue linen dress was the picture of propriety, and she couldn't wait to get it off. "Undo me," she said to Richard, offering him her back.

He leaned over and unzipped the dress, kissing her shoulder blades. "Hungry?" he asked.

"Yes," she said. "Let's do Chinese. Then bowling." She stood up and let the dress fall to the floor, leaving her wearing the cutest cream lace bra and panties. "I need something low brow."

She went into her bedroom to get dressed. I looked at Richard. "You have to work this out."

He nodded. Annemarie returned wearing a denim skirt, a yellow cotton tank top and strappy sandals. "Want to come?" she asked me, slipping a pair of ankle socks into her bag. She was going to look awfully cute in those bowling shoes.

I shook my head. "Work."

"That's right," said Annemarie. "The talent convention." I nodded. Swarms of wannabe singers, actors, dancers, and models were coming into the hotel for the weekend, along with a slew of agents, producers, and other industry professionals. I would be working into the night making croissants and pastries for the Saturday morning breakfast. Already guests were feasting on the delicacies I'd whipped up just a few hours earlier. These upper level conventions where they wanted everything homemade were brutal, but I thrived on them. I loved sweet things of any kind–making them, eating them, savoring them. I looked at Annemarie, who was definitely one of the sweetest people I'd ever known, and Richard, also sweet, but at the moment looking agitated and scared. He'll be all right, I told myself as they waved and scooted out the door.

After they left, I went into my room to get ready for work. I'd showered earlier and put on my white terry robe, which I now slipped off and replaced with white cotton bikinis, jeans, and a T-shirt. I threw my clean cooking clothes into a bag—more white cotton, chinos on the bottom and a button down, short-sleeved shirt on top. In a couple of hours, they would be covered with butter, chocolate, and raspberry stains. Silly thing, to make cooking clothes white. I pulled my long blonde hair into a pony tail and grabbed a hair net for when I got to the kitchen. Roland would be there, as usual, and Jenn. And Chad.

It had been awhile since I longed to see anyone in particular, not for months, since my crush on Richard had gotten way big. I still thought he was hot property, but lately my attentions had been wandering elsewhere. Back when I had it bad for Richard, I tried to drop hints to Annemarie about it. I didn't like secrets between us, but she just wasn't open to hearing it. So I told my good old friend and fuck buddy Jenn about it. She was always happy to listen to my troubles and keep me in orgasms, as long as she wasn't busy with anyone else.

Lately, though, she'd discovered Iona, whom she described as a delicious butch. They met at the body shop where Iona worked. Jenn said Iona had done wonders with her Saab, but nothing compared to what she'd done for her in bed. There would be talk of letting me in on it, but first Jenn had to get her fill of Iona alone. We'd have fun, like always, but for now I had more important things to think about. Like helping Annemarie through her upcoming breakdown. And Chad.

For the last month, Chad had replaced Richard in my fantasies. Ironic, I thought, slipping on my Keds and heading for the hotel. Now that Richard is waffling with Annemarie, I have something better to do. Or at least I hoped I would, and soon.

It was just my good luck that Chad was so responsible. When I arrived at the kitchen, he was there, standing by the door reading a tattered copy of *Anna Karenina*. He barely looked up as I approached, quietly, watching his thick, layered hair fall over his eyes as he peered down at the pages. "Hi, Chad," I said softly, slipping the key into the lock.

"Hey," he answered, without looking up. He folded the page over and put the paperback into the canvas bag slung over his shoulder, then gave me his full attention. "How goes it, Lilah?" The reddish tinge of his lips made them look extremely yummy. He had great teeth, straight and white, and the most incredible dimple in his right cheek. I got a warm feeling inside, thinking about tasting that rosy mouth, and dipping my tongue into the little cavern his dimple made.

"I'm great," I said, communicating more with my eyes than my voice. I loved to flirt, and Chad was the best subject I'd found in ages.

"Excellent," he whispered, answering with a twinkle in his brown eyes. We'd been doing this for awhile. It was great fun, but I thought it was time to move on to the next stage, and my antenna told me Chad was right there with me. The timing may not have been perfect, what with Annemarie's imminent crisis, Richard about to lean on me hard, Jenn's upcoming invitation to join her with Iona, and hordes of entertainment professionals and wannabes about to converge on the hotel. But, hey. It was important to strike when the iron was hot, and judging by Chad's eyes, he was flaming. I smiled at him, parting my lips just a tad. The steam coming off Chad was practically visible. Yeah, he was ready.

We stepped into the kitchen and I turned on the overhead lights. Chad slipped by me, brushing against my backside as he went. In my mind, I said, *You just did that so I could feel your hard-on*. I smiled at him as I stepped into the lounge and quickly changed into my cooking clothes. When I came back into the kitchen, Chad was getting ready to put on his hair net. I pulled mine out of my pocket and joined him. Who'd have thought putting hair nets on could be sexy? But it was, as both of us languidly tucked our unruly locks into the stretchy, web-like structures. Then we looked at each other and laughed, because hair nets sure don't look sexy.

Jenn came in, her bleached bob already tucked into her net. "What's the deal tonight?" she asked, dropping her backpack in the employee closet. "Croissants? Danishes? Muffins?"

"All that," I said.

"Why can't they just order from the damn warehouse?"

I smiled. Jenn's impatience only meant one thing. "Seeing Iona later?"

11

I asked.

Jenn licked her lips and grinned. "Oh yeah," she said, stealing a glance at Chad, who was disappearing into the employee lounge. "You busy tonight?"

They were ready for me sooner than I thought. Chad came out and smiled at me on his way to the sink. So many choices. "I think so," I said.

"Think so?" Jenn looked surprised, and confused, then she saw my slight nod toward the corner where Chad was busily scrubbing his hands. "Ah," she said. "Soon, then?"

"Yes," I answered. "Definitely."

Roland came in with his usual flourish. "I'm here," he cried. "Now we can begin." His sweaty dome of a head was covered in a white baker's hat and he wore his signature black dress shoes which always looked like he'd just had them shined.

"All right," I said. "Let's get to it."

We spent the next several hours mixing, kneading and shaping. At midnight, I thanked everyone for a job well done. I'd be coming back in the early morning hours to bake everything we'd prepared so it would be warm and fresh for breakfast. Jenn ripped off her hair net and left quickly, winking at me as she went. Roland took his time, removing his apron, smoothing and folding it. Chad lingered, spending way too much time in the bathroom as I bade Roland goodnight.

After Roland left, Chad emerged. He'd changed into denim cut-offs, a blue button down shirt, and leather sandals. It was the first time I'd seen him in street clothes. During the months he'd been working with us, he came and went in his whites. The sight was better than I expected—tight, shapely calves and sculpted thighs, generous biceps, and the ripples of a washboard stomach evident through the thin material of his shirt. *Oh Chad*, I thought, *you may be thin, but you are built*. I melted a little at the thought of the jackpot I'd hit. "Hi," I said.

"Hey." It was a whisper, sliding from his lips along with his breath, making the word sound like a quiet, sexy hiss. He smiled, his hand reaching for his hair again, brushing back the bangs that never seemed to stay in place.

"You're all changed," I said.

He nodded. "Want to go out somewhere?"

I pulled off my net, shaking my head so my long, straight hair fell like a fan around my shoulders, and remembered my jeans and T-shirt. "I don't have anything to wear."

"What a shame," he said.

We stood making eyes at each other. There was no awkwardness, no feeling weird, just pure sexual energy flowing between us like an electrical current. "We could go downstairs," I said. "To my roommate's office." Annemarie kept several outfits in her office closet, so she'd be ready for anything. Chad looked confused for a moment, unsure of what I was proposing. "She has extra clothes in there," I said. "I have a key."

"Sure," he said. "And then?"

"Rialto's." It was just the hotel bar, but I didn't want to go far. A drink or two would be nice, and Annemarie's office was close by. Her desk was in a glass house, but there was a connecting room with a couch and a sheepskin rug well broken in by Annemarie and Richard. I'd even used it with Jenn, and a couple of times with the old bartender at Rialto's, who'd moved on to a job in Vegas.

Chad waited in the hall while I let myself into Annemarie's office, where I found the sweetest yellow sundress. It had spaghetti straps and tiny multi-colored flowers. It was completely not my style, but for tonight's purposes, it was perfect. I left my whites, including bra and panties, in a pile on the closet floor, and slipped on the sundress. I put my Keds on top of the dirty whites and found a pair of sandals with a tiny heel. I thought about hitting the bathroom and raiding Annemarie's toiletries, but there was something about the faint smell of sweat mixed with dough that seemed right for this first night with Chad. It was the scent we had courted to, our eyes and hearts locking over butter and flour and cream.

Rialto's was packed, all those music industry wannabes partying hard, hoping to schmooze with someone important. *They are definitely the beautiful people,* I thought as we passed a raven-haired woman in red satin, her luscious breasts heaving from her strapless dress. She was talking to a man with shoulder-length blonde hair, deliciously fleshy lips, and arms adorned with leather and studs. I didn't stop to wonder who they were. No one important would be here. These things just didn't work that way. The wannabes would have to be their own company, and hey, they shouldn't have any complaints about that. They all looked pretty good.

It was noisy and dark in Rialto's, and steamy. No amount of air conditioning could dull the heat created by the masses of drinking, dancing bodies. Fit, barely clad figures undulated wildly under the disco ball, hips and asses shaking and rubbing against one another, hair flying and free. The DJ was spinning some excellent funk that made the dance floor call out to me.

Chad was looking around, checking things out. I tried to read his face, and thought maybe this wasn't what he had in mind. Well, it wasn't what I had in mind either, not for long, but the dance floor might be just the thing before we got down to business, kind of like the appetizer before the main course. I wrapped my hand around Chad's forearm and squeezed. God, it felt good under my fingers, and I took the opportunity to gently stroke his skin as I pulled him toward the dance floor and said, "Come on."

When he realized where we were headed, he smiled, much to my relief. He was worried about sitting down and having a drink, I surmised, since we certainly couldn't talk in there. But dancing was a different thing, another way to communicate. I pulled him into the middle of the floor, making a space for us in the crowd. It wasn't a big space, which was fine with me. It kept us close. The dress may have been perfect for my ultimate plans for the night, but it wasn't great for wriggling arms and thrusting hips. It was too short, and I worried about it riding up and exposing my cheeks. But once I started to relax into the dance, feel the vibrations of the rhythmic bass under my skin, and lose myself in the freedom and wildness of the movements, I began to care less, really, what showed.

Once I was good and in the groove, I turned my attention to Chad, looking to connect my primal motions with his. He was a bit of an awkward dancer, but his enthusiasm made up for his lack of rhythm. There was something genuine and sweet in the way he let go, smiling as his feet stepped this way and that. He wasn't a bit self-conscious, and he was definitely enjoying himself. He smiled brightly at me, as if to say, *This is fun. I'm glad I'm doing this with you.* It wasn't quite the smoldering, my-body-pressed-up-against-his-our-hips-swaying-in-perfect-unison-to-the-music experience I was hoping for, but unlike my dear best friend Annemarie, I could go with the flow.

I resigned myself to a more chaste and wholesome mode of dance-floor flirtation, shimmying my shoulders for Chad, smiling at him until the end of the song. Once, I turned my back to him and slightly bent over as I shook to a funky drumbeat, giving him a momentary glance at my creamy, firm ass, one of my best assets and a source of personal pride.

The funk faded out, morphing into something totally different, something hypnotic and new-agey, but whatever, I didn't care because we weren't staying for it. I pulled Chad off the dance floor and led us out of the hedonistic pleasure den, away from the hungry, horny people desperate for booze and drugs and sex and networking. Next stop, Annemarie's office.

The dancing and the eye contact and the anticipation—it had been way too long since I'd had a good fuckhad gotten me wet and excited. As we stumbled into the quiet safety of the hotel lobby, we were laughing. I was still pulling Chad, this time toward the elevator. "Hey," he said. "Where are we going?"

I turned to him and grinned. "Upstairs," I said. I saw him hesitate, and knew instantly that he didn't want to go. I was crushed. "Why not?" I asked without thinking, my usual finesse and upper-handedness dwindling after the hot dancing and the thought of wrapping myself around Chad.

I let go of his hand. He brushed his hair from his eyes, that thoughtless, habitual little gesture that I found so endearing. "I just—" He paused, looking me so deeply in the eyes that I actually felt flustered. "I thought we could talk."

"Talk?" Definitely not what I had in mind.

"Yeah," he said, rather sheepishly. "We don't get to talk much in the kitchen."

It was true. In the kitchen there was lots of chatting, about the weather, who was staying in the hotel, what movies we'd seen lately, and the latest jokes we'd heard. But it was group talk, never personal. Suddenly I remembered Chad seeking me out in the employee lounge, or in the hall, or at the sink, and how I took it as an invitation to flirt. He was flirting, I realized. He definitely liked me. But he also wanted to get to know me, and I had miscalculated in thinking that we were on the same page. When I was hot for someone, my idea of getting to know the person was a good roll in the hay. Whether we developed a deeper friendship depended on his or her performance in that arena.

Chad didn't want to play it that way. I looked at him smiling at me, a question and a twinkle in his eye. *Are you game? Can you go with me?* I sighed and reached for him, cradling his square chin in my palm. God, he was a sweet guy. There was an innocence about him that was really getting to me. As I caressed his cheek, running my thumb along the slightly damp, cushy flesh of his bottom lip, I felt my poor deprived pussy tingle. Chad answered me with his tongue, darting it along my thumbprint like he was inking it up for an impression.

There was a holding back to it, though, and I felt an aching disappointment followed by a frustrating annoyance. Damn this man who was too much into foreplay and conversation. I had needs. That was something Chad was going to have to learn about me. I wasn't done with him yet, but I was through with him for the evening. My watch said quarter to one. The night was young, and Jenn and Iona were out there. "The dancing was fun," I said. Chad nodded, and I took a moment to laugh with him about it. Then I drew in a long breath and sighed. "I have to get up so early."

He took my hand in his, squeezing it gently. "Okay," he said, looking unconvinced. "Is that all?"

"Yeah," I said. "Really, I'm tired." I started to back away. "Got to go," I said, blowing him a kiss and retreating.

*Good riddance*, I thought. Chad was definitely not the nasty boy I'd been hoping for. He could be a fine plaything, once I taught him a few things. Tonight, though, I was not ready to give up.

As soon as I hit the sidewalk I pulled my phone out of my bag and dialed Jenn's number.

# Chapter 3

# Pleasures of Three

**LILAH**

Jenn picked up on the third ring. "Hey, sweetheart." Her voice was one big purr, laced with ecstasy.

"Where are you?" I asked.

A little moan of surprise, then she answered, "Tied to my bed."

I breathed the summer air deeply, heading as quickly as I could for my car. The night was clear and calm, making the colorful city lights shine brilliantly. It was good to be alive in this beautiful city in the middle of this beautiful night, heading to meet two beautiful lovers. I heard Jenn grunt with astonishment and pleasure. "What's Iona doing to you?"

Assorted *oohs* were all I heard. Seconds passed, Jenn kept moaning, and I finally reached my Honda Civic. "Come on, baby," I said. "Tell me."

"No," said Jenn, panting hard. "Come and see."

I turned the key and pulled out of the garage. "I'm on my way, but stay on the phone."

Another wild wail came from Jenn, and my pussy started to water, imagining what they were doing and anticipating joining them. "Is she licking you?" I asked.

"No." Pant, pant. Moan. "*Ahhhh.*" Her strangled cry sounded almost pained. "Lilah. Oh, baby. Are you almost here?"

I was turning onto Jenn's street. Thank goodness she lived so close to the hotel. "Yeah. I'm coming."

"So—am—I!" I pulled in front of Jenn's building as she climaxed, calling out Iona's name.

"Buzz me in!" I yelled, sprinting up the front steps as the phone went dead. The door started buzzing loudly, and I just managed to grab it and pull it open before it sputtered into silence. Iona was anxious to get back to Jenn, it seemed. Who wouldn't be?

I didn't bother with the elevator, instead ran up four flights to Jenn's apartment and banged on her door, which she opened. "Hey, honey." I was panting and breathless, and not just from hurrying up all those stairs. Jenn was standing before me buck naked, her pale, china doll skin glistening with sweat and who knew what else. The nipples of her small breasts were bright pink and alert, her chest and flat belly heaving with deep breaths, her shaven mound puffed up like a little hill. I could see the enlarged, pinkish bud of her clit blooming from between her crack, a little flower sending tingles down my spine. She stepped away from the door and said, "Come in." When she dropped her hands to her side I noticed the red marks around her wrists. Her clear blue eyes were shining and bloodshot, her rosebud mouth trembling and swollen, but she was smiling, looking a little like the cat who caught the canary.

When I stepped inside, Jenn linked my hand in hers and led me through the messy living room to her bedroom. We stepped over piles of unopened mail, books, and empty takeout containers before entering Jenn's lair. I called it that because Jenn's taste in decorating the most intimate room of her life reflected her inner wild side. She'd painted the walls a deep forest green, and on the two long, vertical windows she hung sheer leopard curtains that let the sun shine in brilliantly every morning, even when you'd been up all night and really didn't want to see it. Faux leopard and tiger throw rugs littered the floor haphazardly. The furniture was deep brown wood, the bed a king size platform crowned by a futon which was always covered with satin leopard sheets, and pillows with multi-colored shams and cases. Seeing Iona sprawled lazily on it, I knew that Jenn had finally found the wild thing her room had been created for.

Iona looked at me with a cockeyed smile and hungry, playful eyes. "Lilah," she said in a husky voice. "What a sweet little flower." I remembered Annemarie's girlish sundress that I had put on for Chad. *Definitely not the right outfit for this situation*, I thought. Apparently I was wrong. "What a lovely dress," said Iona. She was wearing a white ribbed tank top that looked rather alluring spread tightly over her nearly flat chest. Her hair was styled in a neat, barely there buzz cut, her shoulders were broad, her arms taut and powerful looking, her hands rough and work-worn. I looked hard and saw the faintest trace of grease under her fingernails, and was surprised at the flutter it made in my belly. That was nothing compared to the heat that fired in my pussy when I looked at Iona's leather harness and the large dildo it supported. I must have been unable to take my eyes off it, because Iona put her hand on it and stroked it, saying, "You like Daddy's cock."

Jenn giggled and came up behind me, licking my ear and unzipping Annemarie's dress. I could feel my nipples and my clit throb, standing at hot, hungry attention. Jenn's tongue licked the side of my neck, my shoulders, my arm as she pulled the dress down. Then she knelt behind me and slipped it all the way off, kissing and licking the cheeks of my butt. All the while Iona smiled and stroked her big dick.

Jenn placed her hands between my thighs and gently pushed them open. I obliged, standing naked before Iona with parted legs. Jenn began licking my inner thighs, traveling the road to my hot, waiting pussy. Her fingers parted my lips and I knew she was curling her tongue in that way only she could, getting ready to stuff it inside me. She pressed a pink dental dam against me, and I felt her tongue's hotness tunnel into me. The pleasure was unbearably sweet, and I moaned and reached down to hold Jenn's head.

Iona got off the bed and knelt in front of me, moving my hand away from Jenn's head so she had a clear view of her eating me. "That's it, baby," she said. "Clean her out." Jenn started going at me with greater enthusiasm, licking the length of my pussy and taking my clit into her mouth to suck. I began to bounce gently up and down, pressing against Jenn's face. I looked down and watched Iona taking in the sight of Jenn feasting on me. Suddenly Iona turned her head up and our eyes met in one fast, hard, burning connection. It was the most erotic moment I'd ever experienced, and I felt myself explode into Jenn's mouth, my hips bucking every which way and nudging a laughing Iona in the face. Jenn stayed glued to my pussy, letting it gush and throb.

"That was beautiful," Iona whispered as I collapsed onto the floor and hugged Jenn, kissing her deeply and passionately. "But very naughty."

Jenn giggled and said, "Does she need a punishment, Daddy?"

"Oh, yes," said Iona, getting off the floor. "A damn good one." I looked at Jenn questioningly but she just smiled and pulled me over to the bed, which was covered with several wet spots, Jenn's favorite curved vibrator, a wooden paddle, and a bunch of ropes.

"Get on your hands and knees," Jenn whispered in my ear. I did, and turned to look behind me at Iona, who had slipped on a condom and was greasing up her large, protruding cock. My pussy swelled again—something about the sight of Iona rubbing her dick that way was outrageously sexy. She reached for something on the bed and as I turned the other way to see what it was, I caught a glimpse of the paddle being swept off the sheets.

I stiffened. My bare butt, sticking up unashamedly in the air, suddenly felt very vulnerable. I shrieked as the paddle whacked my soft cheeks. I was thin but not sculpted—working out was not my thing—and my lovers were always surprised at the meatiness of my ass. Iona was no exception.

"Oh, lovely," she said, grabbing a hunk of skin in her hand and squeezing until I yelped. I looked back at her devilish face, smiling at me with a finger to her mouth. "Shhh," she whispered. "Take your punishment like a quiet, good girl." The paddle came down again, harder, making my skin tingle and burn at the same time as my pussy throbbed with desire over the sight of Iona wanking her cream-colored cock.

What I really wanted, I realized, was that cock inside me. "Fuck me," I tried to beg, but the paddle hit me again and a garbled, unintelligible moan escaped my lips instead.

"She's liking this, isn't she?" Iona said to Jenn, who was busy pinching and twisting my nipples. Tit play, my sex open and exposed, and the sight of Iona's delicious giant rod left my mouth and pussy watering. I was going out of my mind.

Iona tossed the paddle in the corner and opened the drawer to Jenn's night table, pulling out a rubber glove and putting it on. She greased up the glove, adding more lube to her dick for good measure. My butt cheeks were still singing, but with the paddle out of the way and Iona taking care of business for who knows what, I relaxed for a moment, letting my hips fall down onto my knees in a yoga-like position.

"Get your ass up off the bed," Iona said. "We're not done with you yet." I was surprised at the way my body responded to Iona's command, viscerally and happily. Jenn was leaning underneath me now, taking my hanging breasts into her mouth. Having them sucked in that position was incredibly arousing, but all this play was really feeling like torture to my open, wet pussy.

Just when I thought I couldn't bear it any longer, I felt it—Iona slid her thick rod inside me. It was hard yet flexible, probing my pussy walls wide and deep. I arched my back to open myself up even further, and Iona responded with a massive cock thrust, an agonizingly delicious spear penetrating me. She pumped me slow and long for a few moments, Jenn still working at my breasts, tenderly nursing them, and I felt another orgasm building from way inside.

Then Iona began to part my cheeks and tickle in between them, and suddenly I knew what that greased up finger was meant for. I stiffened again. I'd never had a good experience with anal sex. I craned my head backwards to speak, but as though in anticipation Iona hissed at me, "Quiet! Be still!" and then her finger that had been rubbing and probing my crack slipped into my anus in one swoop.

There was nothing for it but to relax, so I did my best, telling myself to concentrate on the pleasurable sensations of Jenn's expert tongue at my nipples and Iona's ample cock fucking me good. Iona said, "That's it, baby. Just let it happen." Her cock pushed into my pussy, her finger went deeper in my ass. "We're gonna fill you up good."

She mumbled something to Jenn but I was too delirious with shock and pleasure to hear. Jenn stopped playing with my breasts and suddenly I felt a round, vibrating surface pressing into my clit. "We're ready now," Iona said. "Ready to fuck you hard." She started pumping me in earnest, her huge cock ramming me over and over. All the while her finger was sliding in and out of my anus, penetrating deeper with every thrust, and the vibrator whirred on my flaming, engorged clit and lips.

I had never felt so many sensations at once. Iona's cock was finding places in my tunnel that no man had ever discovered, her gloved finger had opened my anus like a surprise, and the powerful buzzing on my clit was driving me over the edge. I came, a massive orgasm that sent fireworks through my whole body. "That's right," said Iona as I bucked hard, slamming my ass into her hips.

I tried to push Jenn's hand away. The strong vibrations against my throbbing clit were too much. I was spent, or so I thought. "No, no, honey," said Iona. "You're going to take more than that."

Again I was forced to let go and open myself to the dildo, the finger, the vibrator relentlessly working my pussy, my clit, my asshole. Again I was surprised at the new dimensions to which I was taken as I came even harder, groaning in ecstatic pleasure.

Iona pulled out of me, took off the glove and tossed it on the floor, then sat on the bed, and in seconds applied a new condom to her cock. She took Jenn by the hair and led her face into her lap. Jenn took Iona's cock into her mouth, and I watched as she sucked it lovingly, until Iona pulled her hair back and looked hard into her eyes. "Sit on me, babe." Jenn straddled Iona's lap and bounced up and down on her until she came, and I found myself picking up Jenn's favorite curved vibrator and rubbing my sopping clit with it, and coming yet again, in unison with Jenn.

It was 4 a.m. when I turned the key to my apartment door and slipped inside. All was quiet. Annemarie's bedroom door was closed. I opened it a crack and peeked in to see her sleeping peacefully in the darkness. There was no hysterical note or message from her in my room, either. Richard apparently hadn't said anything yet.

I showered quickly and put on clean whites, ready to rush over to the kitchen and get the baking done. I'd be home by early afternoon, ready to sleep the rest of the day and into the night. My pussy, my anus, my butt cheeks, my nipples—everything was singing with a mild, pleasurable ache.

Yet I wasn't at ease. As I slipped out the door on my way back to the hotel and reflected on the night—Chad and his sweet, earnest eyes; Iona and her hard, honest, passionate ones—I had this sinking feeling that Annemarie wasn't the only one about to be in trouble.

# Chapter 4
# Trouble in Paradise

**ANNEMARIE**

.I should have known something was wrong. The signs had been there for weeks. Richard and his urgent questions about what marriage would mean for us. His headaches. His waxing philosophical about the future. Then finally, the disaster, that Friday night after what had been just about the hardest day at work I'd ever had.

We'd eaten at Chef Wong's, and I'd devoured my entire plate of Chicken Lo Mein. That wasn't like me. Normally, I'd have a doggie bag that would last for at least two more lunches, but there'd been no time to eat anything at the hotel that crazy afternoon, and maybe, just maybe, I was engaging in a smidge of emotional eating.

The most venerable and important Mr. Zachary Link, CEO of Pomegranate Records, had needed special attention. A hepa filter, plenty of ionized spring water, and organic seasonal fruits were all waiting for him in his room, but there were problems. No organic cotton bedding and towels, for instance. No hypoallergenic pillows. While he was out, I tracked down everything he needed and got it delivered and installed in his suite. Even though he hadn't mentioned it, I made sure to send up some plant-based soap and toiletries. Anticipating things like that saved me work down the line. It also made people happy, and making people happy was my job.

Later, I stopped in to visit Mr. Link to ensure that everything was in order. I expected a well-groomed, long-haired, new age kind of guy in his forties or fifties. Instead I found a blue-eyed hottie who appeared to be at least a decade younger than my estimate. I was rarely wrong, and the mistake threw me, or maybe it was the smile that could have been in a toothpaste commercial. Perhaps the hairless, admirably muscled bare chest that faced me when he answered the door in nothing but a towel. At any rate, the encounter with Mr. Link had upset the rest of my day, occupying my thoughts and leaving me quite annoyed with myself.

Truth to tell, I'd been off for awhile. I chalked it up to the distraction of planning the wedding, but in hindsight, it may have been my subconscious telling me to pay attention to what was going on with Richard. I should have noticed, for instance, that he barely touched the General Gao's Chicken, his favorite Chinese dish prepared to greasy, spicy perfection by Chef Wong.

Instead I was babbling, something I do with the utmost grace and charm to fill up space when things are starting to become uncomfortable, or when the topic of conversation threatens to stray to something difficult. "Reps from the major record companies are in the hotel this weekend," I said between bites of noodles.

"Oh?" Richard was cutting a piece of chicken. He'd cut every chunk of meat on his plate into small bite-size morsels, but he wasn't eating any of them.

"Yeah," I said. "We've even got the CEO of Pomegranate Records." The image of a juicy pomegranate filled my head, along with Zachary Link's statuesque, godlike physique. A hot flush traveled up my neck and into my face. I was glad the restaurant was dark.

The comment seemed to rouse something in Richard, too. "The Eats are on that label."

"Yes, they are," I said politely, even though I hated The Eats. Lilah and Richard loved their loud, bass-heavy music filled with sexual allusions and innuendo. I thought it was in poor taste. I started babbling again, taking the topic of tunes as the perfect opportunity to discuss our wedding music. I'd planned it all—a classical trio for the ceremony, and a swing band for the reception.

After dinner, Richard said he felt too tired to go bowling. That was fine with me, since I was tired, too, and I was in the mood for sex, always a good way to unwind after a hard day. I dragged Richard up to the apartment and into my room, not paying the slightest attention to his clear ambivalence about the whole idea. Why indulge that when I could just fix it?

Richard sat on my double bed, neatly made that morning with clean

Laura Ashley sheets. He loosened his shirt and tie but didn't make any moves to take them or anything else off, not even his shoes. I'd left my flip flops by the apartment door, so I was barefoot. I climbed onto Richard's lap, hiking up my denim skirt as I straddled and hugged his body.

He hugged me back, a little tighter than was comfortable, as I kissed his neck and licked his ear, a move which never failed to get him going. At least it never had before. "Annemarie," he whispered.

"Mmmm?" I asked, planting my mouth on his.

"I'm sorry," he mumbled through my attempt to kiss him.

"For what?" I asked, trying to pull his shirt out of his chinos.

He stopped me and said, "My head aches. I think I should go home."

"Okay," I said, but what I really meant was that he could go home after taking care of me. I'd had a hell of day, and I needed this. The image of Zachary Link popping into my head every so often didn't ease my agitation, either. I needed Richard to help me get rid of it. I put one hand between his legs, covering the mound of his penis and rubbing. I expected to find it hard and waiting, but it was soft.

There was only one thing to do about that. I kneeled down and undid his belt buckle. "Annemarie," he protested. I ignored him and continued undoing his pants, slipping him out of his boxers. Inwardly I was horrified— —terrified, actually—that he wasn't turned on. Suddenly my desire took a backseat to my fear. Given the circumstances, there were more important things than my own orgasm, like making sure Richard was still in my pocket. There was no way he was going to leave until he was at my mercy.

I looked at his flaccid organ and something stirred inside me, an old secret fantasy I'd never been able to fulfill. I put my hand around the base of Richard's drooping sex and looked up at him. "I'm going to suck you," I said.

His eyes lit up, sending a thrill through me. His penis in my hand quivered and I put my mouth around it quickly while there was still time. I drew the soft, cushiony flesh in, stroking it with my tongue. It felt so different than when he was hard. I liked it, but I didn't want it to stay that way, and it didn't. I rejoiced as I felt it quickly turn into a thick, hard rod inside my mouth, a massive erection that tickled the back of my throat. I sucked hard and deep, letting myself open and relax to take in the whole of him.

He put his hands on my hair and pushed my head down. "Suck me," he said with sexy desperation. In no time at all, I could tell he was ready to come, and I felt relieved and excited. I could still make him melt for me. I started to pull away because swallowing was something I just did not do, but Richard kept his hands on the back of my head, pinning me to him. Before I could even think about it, I felt Richard's erection pulse, and thick, warm liquid spurted into my mouth. I struggled to keep from swallowing it, and instead let it fill my cheeks and dribble down my chin as Richard finally relaxed into a heap and let me go.

I felt like crying, kneeling there with come on my face. All I wanted to do was wipe it off, but I wasn't about to use my hands. When I started to reach for a Kleenex from the night table Richard grabbed my wrists and held them. I looked at him, trembling—this was not the Richard I knew—but all I saw in his face was love and gratitude. Then he smiled devilishly and said, "That looks good on you."

I blushed, but at the same time I felt a warm gush between my legs. Richard let one of my wrists go but I dared not move. With his free hand, he cradled my face, gently rubbing his come into my cheeks, tracing my lips with it. He let the other wrist go and lifted my tank top over my head, unhooked my bra, and began rubbing the cream on my breasts and nipples. Richard watched my reaction as he fondled me, as though he was trying to read what was going on inside me.

What was going on inside me? Richard had each of my nipples between a thumb and forefinger, squeezing and pinching in the most delicious way. It was like a tease, because what I really wanted him to do was suck them, which would mean he'd have to lick his own come off me, which was both repulsive and electrifying. Normally, I'd be telling him just what to do, but this was all different. I felt lost and vulnerable. I kept my arms up, as though Richard still held me captive, and in a way, he did. I loved and hated it at the same time, why I didn't know, all I knew was that I didn't want him to stop. "That's good, isn't it?"

"Yes," I said, surprising myself with the uncontrolled moan that followed my answer.

Richard laughed and said, "Get on the bed."

I lay down, still holding my arms above my head, and let Richard pull off my denim skirt and cotton underwear. He parted my legs wide, then went into my closet and came back with several scarves. I'd never allowed anyone to tie me up, and I never intended to let Richard do it, but my aching, wet sex certainly wasn't going to stop him, and at that moment it was speaking way louder than the objections inside my head.

Richard began with one arm, then the other, walking slowly and deliberately around the four poster bed. I watched my favorite purple silk scarf bind my left hand, then a reddish, flowery chiffon one become the rope for my right. Richard was still dressed, and hard again, his erection jutting out of his boxers. It was as hard as I'd ever seen it, the head shining and purplish, pointing straight at me as he secured my feet.

I wiggled a little after he finished, and found that he'd done a good job. I really couldn't get up, at least not without destroying my best scarves. Richard watched me wriggling as he got naked. "You're not getting away, baby." There was a determination and urgency in his voice that I'd never heard before, and while it was a little disturbing, between my legs I was still responding favorably.

"Stay there," he said, as though I had a choice. Richard left the room. Was he going to leave me like this, I wondered, helpless and horny? The direction of his steps made it sound as though he was going into Lilah's room, which is exactly what he did; I saw when he came back. In one hand he held one of those large white feathers Lilah favored. In the other was a purple vibrator with a little rabbit head sticking out the side, and a control panel attached by what looked like an old-fashioned telephone cord.

I knew what those things were for—Lilah liked to show me her sex toys and tell me all about them—but how did Richard know about them? The question was forgotten as Richard began to tickle the lips of my sex with the feather, brushing up and down, side to side, then a quick flutter. I found myself moaning uncontrollably again. Is this what sexual torture did to people? All I wanted was for Richard to plant his sweet lips on my aching crotch, or better yet, just fuck me. Anything for some relief. But, no, Richard just kept teasing me with that exquisitely subtle feather. "Just relax and enjoy it, Annemarie," he whispered in my ear, giving my earlobe a little suck. "You're going to be here for a long time."

Richard positioned himself so he was kneeling over my chest. His erection looked so good, standing straight in front of me like a tree, his black curly bush surrounding it like a little garden. His balls hung low in their sack, which brushed against the skin between my breasts. *Give it to me*, I wanted to scream. *Give it to me now, anywhere.* I leaned forward to try and grab him with my mouth but Richard backed away, laughing. "You want it, baby?" He reached behind and touched between my legs. I felt myself gush with gratitude, as one finger explored my clitoris then slipped inside me. "Annemarie," he said, sighing and trembling. "You're so fucking wet."

Apparently, my instant gratification was not what Richard had in mind. He took his hand away and cradled my breasts in his palm, grabbing the lube in my night table drawer and slathering them up. Then he squeezed them around his erection, making a warm, moist tunnel for sliding in and out. As he fucked my breasts, I watched the tip of his erection slip out of my cleavage then disappear back down. We'd done this before, but never like this, never when I was bound and helpless. It made seeing it so different. I felt a battle raging inside me, the part that wanted to be in charge against the part that knew that letting this moment happen would be exquisite. That part had never really expressed itself before. Why it was coming out now I didn't really know, except that it had something to do with this new, strange, intense Richard. "You like to see that, baby?" Richard asked.

His words made me gush again. "Yes," I cried.

He backed up, sliding his erection along my belly, brushing my reddish blonde bush and the tip of my clitoris with it before sitting cross-legged between my parted legs. He placed his fingers on my mound, pulling it open to completely expose my clitoris, looking into my sex like he was examining it. One finger teased my nub lightly. "I've never seen you so swollen," he said. I closed my eyes and let myself concentrate on nothing but the feel of Richard's fingers finally probing me. "That's right," he said. "Just let go."

A low buzz sounded, and something firm yet flexible was applied between my legs. I opened my eyes and watched as Richard slipped the purple toy inside me, resting the little vibrating ears on my clitoris. He started fucking me with the vibrator, sliding it deep inside me. I came after two thrusts, bucking and banging against Richard's hand, making animal noises of intense pleasure and release. He left the vibrator buzzing inside me and reached up to hug me tight, and as he kissed my face, I was shocked to realize I had drooled. Richard didn't seem to care, just licked it off and continued to lick lower, along my neck, down my belly toward my throbbing sex.

"I want to taste you like this," he said, and began going down on me. I stiffened, taken aback by the intense sensitivity and stimulation on my spent vagina. "Relax," he whispered. He licked me slow and gentle, and in seconds I found myself turned on again, welcoming his tongue on me, sucking me until I came again in his mouth.

I barely caught my breath before he entered me, riding me long and hard. I'd never, ever been fucked like that before—splayed, completely open, my sex drenched and puffy with pleasure.

Richard came again, inside me where I liked it, and when he trembled against me, I felt a rush of joy. His limp, sweating body lay glued to my own, and he whispered that he loved me, and we fell asleep.

When I woke up in the middle of the night, I was untied, and Richard was gone. I knew that was bad, but I just pretended he'd gone home to cure his headache and slumbered deeply and peacefully until well into the next morning.

# Chapter 5
# The Missing Link

**ANNEMARIE**

A call from Carol woke me.

"Annemarie, where are you?" I squinted and looked at the red numbers on my digital clock. *10:58* glared at me. I was supposed to be at work over an hour ago.

"Oh, Carol," I said. "Oh, shit."

"What?" She sounded shocked. Had Carol ever heard me talk like that? Of course not. I wasn't a prude by any means, but I had a professional image to uphold.

"Dammit," I said.

"Annemarie?" Now she sounded both astonished and vaguely pissed off.

"Thanks so much for calling, Carol. I'll be there in fifteen minutes." I hung up. No point in drawing attention to my blunders. Once I returned to normal Carol would forget they ever happened.

I rolled over and sat up, jumping at the buzzing sound that came out of nowhere. It was Lilah's vibrator, kicking into action. I'd nudged the control panel and the phallic, purple object lay jittering on my bed. Mortification went through me. I'd have to return it. I'd have to wash it first. I could do it when Lilah wasn't home. Hopefully she'd never notice its absence. She certainly had enough contraptions to keep her busy. I turned away from it and tried to get back my focus, but there was Lilah's feather, looking demure and innocent on my flowery sheets.

A blush went into my cheeks as I remembered the night before. A feather was so much nicer than a vibrator. Much more subtle, and certainly nicer to look at. The image of Richard fucking my breasts while I watched came into my head, and I felt my sex get warm at the same time that I felt confused. What had we done last night? I had no time to figure it out now, and no time to get cleaned up, really, but I couldn't very well go to work with dried up semen all over me.

I flew out of bed and was in and out of the shower in four minutes, and into a lavender cotton dress with white sandals in two more. My hair was a bit of a mess, but a bun would fix it quickly. A bunch of hair pins and hairspray and a few minutes later, my locks were in a chignon and looking fine. Pearl earrings and necklace and some mauve lipstick would have to do for the rest of the ensemble.

At 11:27 a.m. I was striding into my office, where Carol sat looking through my file cabinet. "What are you doing?" I asked. I hated people going through my files. They inevitably left things out of order.

Carol jumped and let out a little shriek. "My God, you scared me," she said as she turned to face me. She looked a mess. It wasn't that there was a problem with her dress, or her ponytail, or her turquoise jewelry. It was the flustered expression she wore. That kind of thing was deadly in this business. It was why she was below me, and always would be.

"Sorry," I said. "What are you looking for?"

"The receipts for Kirsten Banner's flowers."

"That was a special order," I said.

"I know," Carol cried, a little too loudly.

I dropped my purse on my desk and looked at my phone—twenty five messages. Boy, was I in trouble. "What do you need it for, anyway?"

"She's checking out today, and she says we overcharged her by $50."

I dropped the mail I was sorting through. "Are you serious?" I asked.

"Yes," she said. "I'm trying to find the receipt so I can verify it."

"Carol," I said, dialing the extension to Kirsten Banner's room. "You're wasting your time." Ms. Banner answered on the first ring. "Ms. Banner," I said in my best Hotel Relations Manager voice.

I thought Carol's jaw was going to drop on the floor when she heard me tell Ms. Banner I would see that her bill was adjusted, and that there would be a complimentary arrangement for her next stay. "Why'd you do that?" she asked. "Kirsten Banner is a bitch and I know she's wrong. Her bill said at least $100 for the flowers. There's no way they were less than that."

"Kirsten Banner comes here for business every few months. She stays in the most expensive suite we have and she spends a fortune on room service. I think we can spare a couple of hundred dollars to keep her coming back." Carol pouted at me, which made me laugh. She was an awfully cute girl. "What else is going on?"

Carol sighed and brushed the stray brown hairs from her ponytail away from her face. "Oh man," she said. "502 needs a special ergonomic chair, 223 doesn't like the cots we provided, 187 says they discussed some special lighting with you that wasn't provided. Shall I continue?"

"No," I said. I tossed the mail on my desk to be dealt with later. There was nothing pressing there. "502. That's Zachary Link's suite."

"Oh, yeah," said Carol.

"I'll take care of that," I said. "Can you address the others?"

Carol shook her head at me. "Did you hear what I just said? You think I can do all that?"

"Of course not," I responded. "It's just that Zachary Link is an important guest. He needs to be taken care of right away."

Carol looked as though she was ready to slap me. "I know that," she said with exasperation. "It's been taken care of. He's been out all morning and plans to return in the afternoon to work. I got the chair delivered an hour ago."

My phone rang. "Hello," I said. "Uh huh. I did set that up myself, Mr. Hatchit. Let me come up and see whether we can get it working." I hung up and said to Carol, "He can't work the damn lights. Give me that list." I looked it over, circled the less important tasks, and gave it back to Carol. "Take care of these and leave me reports on all the outcomes. I'm going to deal with Mr. Hatchit."

I spent the next two hours whittling down the list of complaints and requests. The next opportunity I had to look at the clock told me it was 1:38 p.m. I hadn't had a bite all day and I was starving. A few minutes to put away my receipts and phone logs and I'd be ready to take a half hour or so downstairs at the pub. As I was filing, I heard a knock on my office door. "Come in," I said absently, flipping through folders.

I heard the door creak but didn't turn to see who it was. I was about to put the last receipt in the 'Q' folder when a man's voice said, "Hello, Annemarie." I froze. "Or should I call you Ms. Fitch?"

The receipt fell from my trembling fingers into the file cabinet. I coolly slid the drawer closed, turned, and smiled. "Annemarie is fine," I said. "Mr. Link."

He laughed, a sound like chimes ringing. "Call me Zach. Please."

I tried to ignore these pleasantries and get back to business. "Is there something I can help you with?"

"No," he shook his head. "My room is all set, thanks to you." I wasn't going to bother telling him it was Carol who dealt with the chair. He shot me that fantastic smile that lit up his whole face. It really was admirably put together. Square jaw, defined yet rugged cheekbones, strong nose, deep set and intense eyes, and full, shapely lips. And the head of wavy, black hair with the slightly messy look—wow. He was as handsome as Richard. More handsome, possibly. I shuddered at the thought and immediately blocked it out. "I wanted to thank you for sending up the basket of toiletries," he said. "It was really thoughtful."

"Our pleasure," I said, smiling back and hoping that I didn't appear as discombobulated as I felt. Normally, I knew exactly how I appeared. I felt a rush of anger inside. Nothing was going right, lately.

Zachary Link cocked his pretty head and narrowed his eyes at me. "Our?"

"Yes," I said. "Our pleasure. The hotel's."

"Ah," he said. "I see." He folded his arms over his button down shirt, open just enough to show the smooth, tan skin around his collarbone and the top of his chest. The shirt was spectacular on him—salmon-colored silk, casual yet distinctive. And putting it on top of black, drawstring lounge pants and clogs was a daring move that worked fantastically well. "Have you eaten yet?"

"Actually, I was just about to get a bite," I said.

His eyes smiled. "Would you like to have lunch with me?"

It certainly wasn't the first time I'd been asked out by a guest. Whether I went depended on the guest. Some of the old men who asked just wanted the pleasant company of a younger woman. Some of them wanted more. Saying yes was exactly the right thing to do for the former, and graciously declining was appropriate for the latter. I could always read which was which, and I had only been wrong once, when a female executive from a plastics company turned out to want more than chit chat. But my antenna told me that neither of these two simplistic choices—an arm ornament or a quick roll in the hay—applied to Zachary Link. What the hell did he want?

My heart was thumping surprisingly hard as I stood there trying to decide what to say. "I'm sorry," I spat. "Maybe another time."

He looked stricken and began to blush. "No, I'm sorry. I've put you in a bad position."

His face was actually turning red. This was about the worst thing that could happen to a Hotel Relations Manager. Pissing off a guest was bad, but embarrassing one was unforgivable. I felt my own cheeks begin to turn shades of pink. "No, really, you haven't." I shook my head vociferously. "Really." He stood there looking sheepish. It was sweet—and funny.

I laughed, which turned out to be just the right thing to do. He relaxed and laughed back, and in a minute we were both holding our sides. "Why is this so hilarious?" I said.

"Really," he answered. "You'd think we were still in high school." My breath caught and I stopped laughing. Zachary Link looked into my eyes and I thought I'd dissolve into a puddle on the floor.

"I'm going to Plato's," I said, turning away from him to pick up my purse. "You couldn't go there, anyway."

"What makes you say that?" He seemed dismayed at my change of mood.

"Your allergies," I said. "There are probably very few places you can eat." I could feel the edge in my own voice and the intention to be cruel. Needless to say, doing this to a guest of the stature of Zachary Link was beyond unprofessional.

I was about to apologize when he said, "Actually, I can eat anywhere I want." Chalk up a few more brownie points for Annemarie! Embarrass him, then make him mad!

"I'm sorry. That was uncalled for." We were both quiet for a moment. "I'm having a bit of a hard time lately." I had some damage control to do, and the sympathy ploy was always a good way to go. I decided to throw in a little honesty, too. "Besides, I'm just not sure how to act with you."

"I'm having the same problem," he said. "Given your position, it's not been easy. Now, if I had a crush on, say, a woman in my yoga class, that would make things a lot simpler."

"I'm engaged," I said, flashing my left hand, wondering how he could fail to notice the rock which Richard had bought me. It was the best looking diamond around—I'd picked it out myself.

"And I'm married," he said. "My wife's the one with the allergies."

"And you want to take me to lunch?" Talk about shock. I felt like I'd been hit over the head with a very large, stuffed pocketbook. "Where's she going? The health food store?"

"She's not here," he said flatly. "She was going to come, but it turns out she couldn't make it this weekend."

"How convenient for you," I said. I was starting to feel like I couldn't breathe and realized it was my attempt to hold back tears. Crying in front of the same guest whom I'd just embarrassed and angered—that would be the crowning glory for the day, and I sure wasn't going to let it happen. "Look," I said, sucking in my breath and forcing myself into composure. "I really have work to do. I'm just going to order a sandwich and eat it in my office. You let me know if there's anything you need during your stay, okay?"

He started to say something, then thought better of it. I wanted nothing more than to shout, *What? What is it?*, but I held my tongue. "All right, Annemarie." He practically whispered the words, though it felt like they were floating right next to my ears.

Then he left, quickly and quietly.

I called Plato's and ordered a turkey club, then sat at my desk and dialed Richard's number. The machine answered. *Hey, it's Richard. Leave a message. Ta-ta.*

"Hi, baby," I said into the phone. "How's your head? I'll be done here in a few hours and I'm going to come over and give you a great big massage."

The rest of the day was uneventful, and I had everything wrapped up by 4:45. I tried calling Richard, but he didn't answer his cell. I texted him and still got no response, so I got into my Volvo and drove the twenty minutes to his apartment building, but he didn't answer the door. I assumed he was working out at the gym or on a bike ride, and I headed home where I found Lilah in the living room, her feet up on the coffee table, sipping one of her exotic teas out of her favorite mug, a brown, misshapen one made by one of her old boyfriends. "Hi, love," she said. "How are you?"

I kicked off my sandals and sat next to her, putting my head on her shoulder. "I'm bad," I said.

I felt her body stiffen. "Why?" she asked.

"Why do you think?"

"I don't know," she answered a little too nonchalantly.

I sat up and looked at her. She was so full of shit. "You know something."

"Crap, Annemarie," she said, taking a sip of tea. "What makes you say that?"

"You really think I'm stupid, don't you?" I said, shaking my head. "And another thing. How does Richard know about your sex toys?"

She barely had enough time to swallow before guffawing. "He told you about my toys?" I started blushing for the second time that day. I hadn't meant to say anything about the feather and the vibrator, at least not yet. I was going to think about how to do it, but my face might as well have been a billboard, broadcasting the whole sordid tale. "So that's where my bunny went!" she said.

"Your bunny?" I laughed. "That's the silliest thing I've ever heard. How can you miss it, Lilah? You have so many."

"That one's my favorite," she said.

"Is that what you told Richard?" I asked, cuddling up to her again.

"Mmm, hmm."

"But why were you talking about sex?" I wasn't too worried about cheating, but something felt off. For the most part, I trusted both Richard and Lilah. They were both attractive and sexy, and I knew they admired each other, but I didn't think they would engage in anything behind my back. Lilah had a one track mind about sex and talked about it to everyone, so that wouldn't be unusual. Normally, I'd have no interest whatsoever in their little discussions. But in the course of a day, it seemed, everything had ceased to be normal. I wanted to know what Richard had said. It seemed more important than ever now.

"We talk about a lot of things," said Lilah.

"What has he said about me?" I asked.

Lilah put down her mug and turned to look at me. "What's he told you?"

I felt a chill in my gut. Something was definitely wrong, and I was going to be the last to know. "Nothing," I cried. "Absolutely nothing." Lilah shook her head and looked annoyed. A hollow sense of desperation was forming inside me. "What has he told you?"

"Not much," she said. "He's confused, honey."

"About what?"

"I don't really know. Marriage is a big step, that's all."

"He doesn't want to do it, does he?" I could hear my own voice, high-pitched and hysterical. Thank god it was only Lilah in the room.

She hugged me. "I wouldn't go jumping to any conclusions," she said. "And besides—" She pulled away and looked at me again. "Can you tell me you're one hundred percent sure?"

I remembered Zachary, the electricity in the room with him, messing with my carefully laid plans. What, exactly, did *that* mean? "Who is?" I asked. "Who ever is?"

Lilah picked up her tea and held the cup high as though making a toast. Her smile was wry and maybe even bitter. "Amen," she said, and gulped the scalding liquid. "Amen to that."

# Chapter 6
# The Unraveling Begins

**LILAH**

If I didn't know Richard so well, I'd say he was a real asshole. When Annemarie came home from work on Saturday night, looking for all the world like a forlorn, lost little girl, I thought maybe he'd talked to her.

But as she parked her pretty butt on the couch next to me and cuddled in, I knew the coward hadn't said a goddamn word.

That was bad enough. Then he had to make it worse by calling me. I was lying on my futon, enjoying a good Sunday afternoon sleep. I had to hit the kitchen later, and I needed my rest. Annemarie was at the hotel, seeing that the weekend guests were leaving happily and efficiently. "Hello," I breathed into my cell.

"Hey," said Richard. "Did I wake you?"

"Yes," I said, and for good measure, added, "You jerk."

Normally, he would have laughed. Shooting teasing insults at each other was one of the ways we harmlessly flirted. It helped diffuse the sexual attraction between us. Not this morning. "You ignored all my texts," he said defensively. Then all the air went out of his sails. "I'm sorry, Li. God, I'm sorry."

"Chill," I said. "It's all right. As long as you and your sweet cheeks call Annemarie."

Silence on the other end. Uh oh. Normally, the compliment would have gotten a husky chuckle, a response in kind, a conspiratorial whisper. I rolled over, letting my naked body rub against my favorite velour sheets. I wished Richard wasn't calling with such serious business. We could have had a nice, randy conversation, then I could have used my favorite vibrator, except I couldn't because Annemarie hadn't returned it yet. She'd asked whether she needed to boil it before she gave it back, but I said no, just wash it, boiling will mess up the batteries. She looked a little dismayed, and apparently was still trying to figure out how the hell to sterilize it. I'd have to get on her. I wanted my bunny back.

Only one night had passed since my romp with Jenn and Iona. It had left me in a perpetual state of wetness. Focusing on that allowed me to ignore trying to figure out what kind of serious situation Jenn had gotten herself into, what the hell was going to happen with Chad, how Annemarie was crashing, and whether I was going to be able to keep away from Richard, which was all to the good. Focusing on things never helped. Let go and trust the universe, that was my motto.

Right now there would be no fun, however. Richard, silent on the other end of the phone, obviously expected me to talk. "Sweetheart," I whispered. "What kind of position are you trying to put me in?"

"Damn it, Lilah," he said. "I need someone to talk to."

"Don't you have any friends, big boy?"

Richard made a funny sound, a muffled laugh or cry, I couldn't tell which. "You can't talk to guys about this stuff."

"Okay," I said. "What stuff?"

"Meet me somewhere."

He was pleading, and damn if it wasn't totally appealing. Uh oh again. "I don't know."

"Come on, Lilah," he said, a bit more assertively. "I need you."

"All right. But I'm going to tell Annemarie."

"After we meet, okay? I don't want her showing up."

"Fair enough," I said. "But I'm doing it for her, okay?"

"Of course," said Richard. "We both are."

We made a plan to meet for lunch on Monday at Patty Pete's, a chain restaurant Annemarie despised. I fell back to sleep for a few more hours.

When my alarm went off, I slipped out of bed and into my jeans, heading for the kitchen where Jenn and I had the graveyard shift. The air was still and hot and damp as I walked to work. Tropical and steamy, like everything in my life at the moment, it seemed.

The hotel was quiet in the middle of the night. Rialto's was closed and the beautiful people were gone. Next weekend, a convention of some group called Mothers of Preschoolers was coming, sans children, for pampering, apparently. I thought fleetingly about what that might be like— married with kids, and a steady man. A microscopic part of me could see the joy in it, but the minute I thought of Jenn and Iona and Chad and Richard and Annemarie, all the riches in my life I was enjoying and those yet to be discovered, the idea of marriage and family life paled.

When I got to the kitchen, Jenn was waiting in the hall, leaning against the wall in her whites and hair net. "Hey." She looked worn out, her pale face free of makeup, subtle gray half-moons under her eyes. Being tired didn't interfere with the aura of deep satisfaction and sensuality she emitted. I'd seen Jenn well fucked before, but never like this, never looking so raw and exposed and real.

I kissed her cheek. "Hi, love. You ready to make the donuts?"

She giggled. "Whatever you say, boss." We never made donuts, but the line was a little joke between us. This morning we were making bread and the dessert specials for the restaurant—chocolate truffle cake and my personal favorite, key lime pie.

We took turns at the sink. I couldn't help but watch Jenn's pert butt, sticking out ever so slightly as she scrubbed her hands. I flashed back to the other night, an image of Iona's meaty dildo, and I thought of it penetrating Jenn's tender openings. My pussy swelled. I stepped up behind Jenn and took a chunk of her ass cheek in my hands. She winced. I was taken aback. "You all right?" I asked.

"Oh, yeah," she said, smiling and drying her hands. "Just a teensy bit sore." Iona must have gotten a little out of hand with her paddle, or her hand, or who knew what else.

I prepared the cake batter and Jenn put the bread ingredients into the kneading machine. "What's up for this afternoon?" I asked. It wasn't unusual for us to have a daytime rendezvous, given our strange hours.

"I'm cooking," she said.

"Cooking? You mean, like we're doing now?"

Jenn laughed, a sound like tiny, tinkly bubbles emerging from her pretty throat. "No, silly. I'm making dinner for Iona. Gazpacho and salad and rice pudding."

"Interesting combination," I said.

"Mmmm," Jenn answered. "She's a vegetarian."

Something was definitely going on. Jenn didn't cook, except for work, which wasn't really cooking, it was creating delicacies to nurture the sweet tooth and the soul. It had nothing to do with nutrients or health or anything like that—it was pure comfort and pleasure. Gazpacho was not a comfort food, or a pleasure food, although my experience with Iona told me she was no stranger to those concepts. Cooking for a person in the way that Jenn planned to cook for Iona meant something. I'd never seen Jenn so smitten. I was surprised at the hot flash of jealousy that coursed through me, but I chalked it up to the fact that I just needed some sex—for the last two days I'd been hot and horny for another session with Jenn and Iona. "Iona's coming over after work?" Jenn nodded, carefully placing the last ingredient into the machine and turning it on. "Want some company?"

She hesitated, and for a moment I thought it was because she was concentrating on her work. Then she said, grudgingly I thought, "Sorry, baby. Not tonight."

Now it wasn't just a tiny flash of jealousy I felt. I was pissed off. What was I, some sort of plaything to be summoned when they felt like adding spice to their fucking? The intensity of my feelings shocked me. I wasn't like this. My anger dissipated, followed by a wave of panic. What the fuck was happening to me? Jenn touched my arm. "Hon," she whispered. "You okay?"

"Yeah," I said.

Jenn took my answer at face value and proceeded to let loose on what she was clearly dying to gab about. She'd never cooked for Iona before—I didn't bother pointing out that she never cooked for anyone—and she was nervous and excited. As soon as she got home, she was going to clean her whole place. Clean? Another bomb dropped, but Jenn didn't skip a beat. Once she had her place clean, she said, she'd set to work setting up the sweetest little candlelight dinner for two. Her eyes were burning when she started talking about the after dinner reward she expected to receive. She turned to me, breathless. "Oh, Lilah. I've never met anyone like her."

"Neither have I," I said, with only a little sarcasm.

Jenn looked stricken. "Don't you like her?"

I was at a crucial point in the chocolate truffle batter. "Hold it," I said. Jenn waited patiently. She knew what kind of concentration my creations required. I was glad for the breather. It gave me time to settle my emotions. Once the batter was finished, I turned to Jenn. "I enjoyed her," I said. "A lot. But I don't know her, so how do I know if I like her?"

Jenn looked annoyed. "A person can tell about someone. You fucked her, Lilah. Didn't you get a feeling about her?"

I had, of course. She was a serious person, intensely grounded. She reminded me, I suddenly realized, of Chad. If you looked at the way they lived their lives, the two of them couldn't have been more different, but they shared a vibe of some kind, a vibe that a week ago I would have said was dull and uninteresting. The truth was that Iona fascinated me, and not just because she was an amazing fuck. And Chad—the thought of him made me want to cry. I realized I'd been pushing him out of my mind with thoughts of Jenn and Iona, and truth to tell, Richard, but my lingering feelings of warmth and wetness had just as much to do with him as any of the others. I turned to Jenn and hugged her. "I'm sorry, hon," I said. "I'm just jealous, you know."

Jenn laughed uncomfortably. "Seriously?" she whispered.

I realized the message she might be getting—that she'd been confused about our relationship, and I'd wanted something more from her than our dear, fun, sexy, little friendship, which I didn't think was true. "Yeah," I said, nudging her hard. "Because I wanna get laid tonight."

"Since when are you at a loss for a lover?" she asked. Then she said, "We'll get together again, soon. I promise." Somehow, that didn't make me feel better.

We spent the rest of the shift working diligently. Just as I was finishing the clean-up, Annemarie burst in looking like someone had just died in a car accident. "Lilah," she cried. Jenn, who'd left the kitchen to clean up, stepped out of the ladies room. She'd changed into a tight, hot pink mini dress and flip flops. Her bleached bob was unbrushed and wild, and her face was still pale and natural except for the vibrant pink she'd smeared across her puffy lips. Annemarie composed herself immediately, nodding hello at Jenn.

Jenn smiled wickedly at Annemarie. "Hey, girl," she said. "Long time no see." Jenn had been hot for Annemarie forever, even though I told her more than once to forget it, the chick was straight as an arrow and committed, and if anyone was going to bed her, it would be me. None of that prevented Jenn from flirting. I was glad to see that Iona hadn't completely wiped out the Jenn I knew and loved.

Annemarie knew men, but she had no clue about women. I theorized it was just denial—she didn't want to think about a woman looking at her that way. "Hi, Jenn," she said, more than a little distracted.

Jenn kissed my cheek and said, "Bye, sweetie." Then she waved and winked at Annemarie, turning her mouth into the sexiest little 'o' shape when she said, "Toodle-o."

As soon as the door closed, Annemarie started sobbing. She was talking a mile a minute, but I couldn't understand a word. "Slow down," I whispered, stroking her hair. "I don't know what you're talking about."

She tried to compose herself. After a brief bout of hyperventilating, she managed to choke out, "He's gone, Lilah."

"Where?" I asked. We both knew we were talking about Richard.

She shook her head, wiping the tears from her face and smudging mascara all over her cheeks. "I don't know," she whispered.

"Come on," I said, pulling her into the ladies room. "Let's get you straightened up." I wiped her face with a moist kitchen towel and sat beside her as she told me the whole sad tale. He hadn't answered his phone or texts all weekend. Annemarie had even emailed him. The word at his office was that he'd be out for a few weeks due to a family emergency.

"What could be wrong?" Annemarie said, to the universe as much as to me.

"It's gonna be all right," I whispered. Inwardly, I was furious with Richard. Annemarie had no clue what was up. For all she knew someone in Richard's family was deathly ill. Heck, Richard himself could be dying and she was stuck with no contact and no information. It was downright despicable of him. I thought about telling her that I was meeting Richard in a few hours, but I couldn't. It was either betray Richard or betray Annemarie. I told myself that I'd speak to Annemarie about my contact with Richard tonight, regardless. He was getting this one inch and nothing more.

"What time is it?" Annemarie said as if she were just waking up from a fog.

"A little after nine."

Abruptly, she turned into a different person, jumping up from the couch we'd been sitting on and looking around frantically. "Oh, god," she said. "I have to go." She smoothed her hair then added, "To work." She looked at me, unbelievably composed despite the fact that her make-up was completely off and there were tear stains on her dress, but that was Annemarie all over. She was a marvel.

I stood and hugged her. "See you tonight, okay?"

She smiled. "Yeah," she said. "Gotta go." I shook my head, perplexed. She was acting for all the world like she was on her way to something she was excited about. Custom flower arrangements? Special menus? Arranging an escort for some rich asshole? Enough, already. I ignored it. There was altogether too much unusual behavior being exhibited by my closest friends without adding Annemarie to the list. I slung my bag on my shoulder and headed home to shower before lunch with Richard.

# Chapter 7
# The Meeting

LILAH

Patty Pete's was a dive and the perfect place to meet Richard, because even though it was near the hotel, Annemarie would never step foot in it. I seated myself at a table, sinking into a plastic chair the color of astro turf to wait. The waitress, a teenager dressed in denim shorts, white ankle socks, garish red sneakers, and a white T-shirt with "Patty Pete's" emblazoned in a crimson-colored logo, came over to the table and handed me a menu. "Thanks," I said.

"Sure," she answered. When she smiled, I could see a pink wad of bubble gum at the side of her mouth.

"Wait," I said as she turned to leave. "Another menu, please."

"You waiting for someone?"

Duh, I thought. There was a reason the girl was working here. "Yes," I said, peering at the door, which Richard was in the process of opening. "He's here."

The waitress dropped another menu on the table and walked off. I waved until Richard saw me. I'd picked a corner, attempting to get as much privacy as possible.

Richard was looking mighty fine, if a bit frantic. He'd let his thick mop of hair go, so instead of looking perfectly styled and controlled, it appeared wild and unruly. One reason for that, I noted, was the bike helmet tucked under his arm. He was wearing black stretchy bike shorts, matte, not shiny. They showed off the bulge of his cock nicely, not to mention the cute rounded muscles just above his knees. Too bad about the baggy T-shirt, which hid his beautiful biceps. Then again, he always hid them. I only knew they were there because I'd seen him wrapped in nothing but a towel, scurrying from our bathroom into Annemarie's bedroom after a shower. "Hi, Ricky," I said.

It was my pet name for him. He wiped the sweat from his forehead. The bike helmet had made a thick red line across it. "Hey," he said, sounding defeated.

"Bike ride wear you out?" He shook his head and started playing with the salt shaker. In my peripheral vision I saw the gum-chewing waitress heading our way. "What do you want?" I asked.

"Nothing."

"We're here. We have to get something." He just shrugged, so I ordered for both of us. A tuna melt with onion rings instead of fries for Richard and a broiled chicken sandwich for me. When the waitress left again I said, "So talk."

He took a deep breath and continued to swivel the salt shaker around. Tiny crystals fell onto the table. Richard ignored them. "I want to marry her," he said.

"Okay," I answered. "The but comes next, right?"

He shook his head. "No buts. I really want to marry her." Richard let go of the salt shaker and it tipped over onto the red and white plastic tablecloth. "You have no idea how much I love her, Lilah."

I had never seen anyone so sincere. For the second time that day, I felt jealousy well up inside me. It made me want to cry, but only for a second. Then it made me angry. "You have a funny way of showing it."

Richard slapped the table. "Damn it, Li. Why do you have to be so fucking hard on me?"

I laughed out loud. "Me? Hard on you? Too bad I didn't have a video camera this morning when Annemarie came into the kitchen. That way you could have seen the look on her face."

That hurt him. He looked into his lap and shook his head. He was doing that a lot. "I just need time."

"For what? To sow your wild oats? To fuck a few girls before the big day?"

"Christ, Lilah, I'm not an asshole."

The waitress came to our table with water. "Well, you're acting like one."

"Fuck you, Lilah," he said. "I thought you were my friend."

The waitress looked unperturbed. "Your lunch will be out in a minute," she said, with the same plastic smile and wad of gum showing. Then she was gone again.

I turned to Richard, who was not being any fun at all. I didn't want to help him with Annemarie. I would have liked nothing better than to take him home and get my hands on the body I'd glimpsed so few times and coveted so many. I had to ask myself — *what kind of person did that make me?* Not a melodramatic one, that's for sure. After just a few days of this run around with Richard and Annemarie, I'd had enough melodrama to last awhile. I put my hand on Richard's, slipping my fingers into his until they were intertwined. "I am your friend," I said. "But I'm Annemarie's friend, too, and she's getting the raw end of this deal."

"It's not that simple," he whispered.

"Oh?"

"She won't listen," he said. "She's so damn stubborn. She likes everything a certain way." He got a faraway look in his eye and a small smile came to his lips. Here he was, talking about what drove him crazy about his girlfriend, and he sounded like he was lavishing compliments on her. "I know she's doing it for me. For us. It's—" he paused. "It's protective. She's thinks she's taking care of our relationship."

I raised an eyebrow. "And she's not?"

He smiled. "Well, she is in a way. It's sweet, and I like to see her authority. But ultimately, it keeps us down."

"How so?"

"I want us to be together but free. I want us to be able to express everything about ourselves." He started looking smug and a little too sure of himself. "There's so much in Annemarie, and she doesn't let herself express it."

"Richard," I said as the waitress put down our sandwiches. "You sound like a girl. Why don't you admit what this is about? You want to fuck other women."

"I admit it," he said, looking me hard in the eye. I let his look sear into me, tell me without words that yes, he wanted to fuck me, too. I acknowledged it with my own eyes, and squeezed his hand. "The thing you don't get, Lilah," he said, "is that there's more to it than that."

"Only if you want to talk bullshit," I said. "Personally, I'm into straight talk." I popped an onion ring in my mouth and grimaced. "God, these are greasy."

Richard tried one. "I think they're excellent," he said.

"What do you know? You like that horrible Chinese chicken thing." Thankfully, the mood had lifted an iota. Food does that. We chatted and ate for awhile. After my last bite of chicken sandwich I said, "So, what's the plan from here, chief?"

"Will you talk to her for me?" he said.

I sipped my water and tried to figure out how to break it to Richard that I had no interest in being his go-between. "Ricky," I said, holding his hand again. It felt warm and strong. When I stroked the skin between his thumb and index finger, he answered back by circling his thumb around my palm, urgent and sweet. I took a deep breath and whispered, "I'm not going to be your spokesperson." I surprised myself with the tears I felt welling up behind my eyes. For Lord's sake, what did I have to cry about?

"I'm not asking you to be," he said, his brown eyes glowing like he was having the same problem. At least he had a reason. "I know I have to tell her myself."

"So what do you want me to do?" I was whispering again, letting my voice fall into a low, husky, sexy murmur. I just couldn't help myself. I didn't usually see Richard this way—all sweaty and macho—and it was damn hot.

He smiled, his light-hearted, flirty smile, thank goodness. "Just tell her I'm okay, I love her, and she shouldn't change any plans."

"You think she's going to be happy with that?"

"No. But it's all I can do right now."

The waitress came back. "Anything else?" she asked, dropping the check on our table before waiting for an answer.

"No, thank you," said Richard, watching her butt wiggle in her shorts as she turned and walked away.

"Don't tell me you're interested in that," I said.

He looked startled as he turned back to me. "In what?"

"Forget it." Maybe I was just projecting. I was the one who thought she was cute. "So, I'm supposed to take care of Annemarie while you figure your shit out."

"Lilah," he said. "You're not supposed to do anything. I'm asking for your help." He looked at me in the most imploring way. I felt my pussy, ridiculously wanting of late, tingle.

"She's my best friend, you know," I said, for my benefit as much as his. "That's why I came to you."

"The only reason?" I asked, raising an eyebrow. Our eyes locked again. More tingles.

"No," he answered, keeping his dark gaze fixed on mine. My mind went into automatic pilot, trying to figure out how I could fuck Richard and stay true to Annemarie. It wasn't conscious or anything—it was just happening. Then Richard said, "You're my friend, too."

"That's it?" I asked. "Just friends?" I was pushing it, I knew. If it happened, I'd figure it out with Annemarie later.

Richard smiled at me. "You're too much for me, girl," he said.

I laughed. "I hardly think so."

Richard was laughing, too, showing his gorgeous teeth. "Someday, Li. Someday, maybe."

We left our money on the table and walked to the door together. I stood by as Richard put on his helmet and leaned over to unlock his bike, giving me a great view of his incredibly developed buttocks. I reached out and gave them a quick pinch. "Lilah!" He jumped, then smiled and gave me a long, hard hug. I didn't know whether to be happy or frustrated by the beginnings of the hard-on I felt when we embraced.

I pulled away and kissed him quickly on the lips. "Take care of yourself, Ricky," I said. He nodded. "When will we see you again?"

"Soon," he said. "Very soon." Then he got on his ten-speed and rode into the bustling city afternoon.

I watched him from behind as he sped beside a row of cars at a red light, zipping past them to the intersection, free and unfettered on his two wheels.

He lifted his body off the seat for a moment to pump harder uphill, then disappeared around a corner.

I turned and walked the other way, heading for home.

The apartment was empty and lonely when I arrived mid-afternoon. I spent an hour in my room, on my yoga mat, stretching like my life depended on it, and it kind of did.

I was going a little crazy, feeling like I was losing hold on reality, what had always been my reality, anyway. Richard taking off didn't surprise me—I had seen the tension that Annemarie refused to acknowledge—but something about it was disturbing me, and I had no idea why. Was it just guilt that I wanted to fuck him and probably would have if he'd been game?

Nah. I didn't do guilt. And if I ever came close, my honesty took care of it for me. Besides, I hadn't bedded Richard, so there was nothing to feel guilty about. I remembered the way he looked at me in the restaurant, full of longing and courage. He was going out on a limb with his whole life, being true to himself and hoping it would all work out. Something about that got to me.

It made me think of Chad. Now that was a real puzzler. But there he was in my mind's eye, floppy brown hair swinging loosely in front of his face, obscuring his mysterious eyes. Maybe I hadn't been focusing on them enough. Maybe the way his hair swooped across them had made me focus too much on his full, fleshy lips and what I wanted them to do to me. I thought back to our first date, and felt a sting over his rejection of me. But he hadn't rejected me, really. He liked me, that much I knew. Why didn't he want to fuck me, then? It was beyond my comprehension that anyone would be turned on by someone and not want to jump in the sack as soon as possible.

While I was thinking about when Chad was next on the schedule—Thursday, three days away—Annemarie arrived home. I heard her key in the door and stepped out of my bedroom. "Li," she exclaimed, leaning one hand on the hall wall and untying her sneakers.

"Hard day?" I asked. Something was definitely awry. She hadn't gone to work, that was certain. Not in shorts and sneakers, anyway.

"Yeah," she whispered. There was a faraway look in her eye that I hadn't seen before.

I moved closer and put my arm around her. "You okay?"

She wrapped one arm around me and we walked into the living room together. "I am," she said. "Yeah. I am."

Annemarie was not acting normally. She should have been letting loose, sobbing into my arms, and asking me what the hell she was going to do. Then I was supposed to tell her that everything was going to be fine, that Richard loved her and was going to come back when he was ready, and that it wouldn't be long. Instead she seemed calm. Where the hell had she been all day? She sat on the couch, pulled off her socks, and put her feet up on the tan ottoman. I positioned myself on the floor and began to give her a foot massage. "Annemarie," I whispered.

"Hmmm?" she asked absently.

"Are you sure you're okay?"

"Mmmm," she answered, sounding bizarrely satisfied.

"What did you today?"

"Work," she whispered.

"Bullshit," I said. "You don't dress like that for work."

She looked at me and smiled wickedly. "I'll tell you mine if you tell me yours."

"What's that supposed to mean?" I asked.

"What do you know?" she said.

"About what?"

"Stop playing games. You know exactly what I'm talking about."

I took each of Annemarie's pretty toes between my fingers and rubbed them. "Why are you so sure I know something?"

"That feels good," she said, leaning forward as I rubbed a spot on the ball of her foot. "Yes. Right there." She settled back down and said, "Because you two like each other. In more ways than one."

I felt myself blush. I hadn't ever felt like Annemarie was open to hearing about my feelings for Richard. Apparently there was no need to tell her. I panicked at the sudden thought that Annemarie might think I was the reason Richard had disappeared from her life. "You think something is going on with us? Me? And Richard?"

"Of course not. I trust you," she said, glaring at me with hard eyes that held the hint of a threat. "But I'm not stupid."

I was feeling pretty stupid at the moment. "Why didn't you ever say anything?"

"Why would I do that?"

"Because you're my best friend," I said. "And we talk about everything."

She looked at me. "Lilah, you talk about everything. You tell me about every person you fuck, and every toy you own. I've never been like that."

I had to admit, she was right. I was Miss Open and Carefree, and she wasn't. Why would I think she'd let on if she knew Richard and I had the hots for each other? Keeping it all in the dark was part of the mechanism she used to stay in charge. "That's true," I said. "Your style is to manipulate people through silence."

She took her feet off the ottoman and planted them on the floor, while using one hand to take her gorgeous red locks out of their bun. "Don't pass judgment, Lilah. We're just different." She shook her long hair so it fell around her pale shoulders, accentuating her ridiculous beauty.

I stayed on the floor, sitting cross-legged, rubbing my own feet. "No question about that," I said.

"Please tell me about Richard."

"I saw him today at his request. I agreed on the condition that I would tell you about it." A look of pain crossed her face and her eyes filled up. "Honey," I said. "We met at Patty Pete's."

"What did you do there?" Now tears were streaming down her face.

"We ate. And talked."

"You ate that abominable food." She shook her head.

I ignored her. "Richard wants you to know that he's okay, that he loves you, and that you shouldn't change any plans."

She was crying hard now, gasps punctuating her wild rant. "I shouldn't change any plans? Who the fuck does he think he is? He can do whatever the fuck he wants, and I just twiddle my thumbs and wait?" She buried her head in her lap and sobbed.

I stroked her hair. "I know it sucks," I said. "But it's all going to work out."

Her voice sounded muffled and strange. "What makes you so sure?"

"Because I know Richard."

She lifted her head and put her tear-stained face close to mine. "And me?" she said. "What about me? What makes you think you know me so well?"

Her breath, smelling faintly of mint, landed hot on my mouth. She kept her face completely still, close and warm next to mine. I had never wanted to kiss her so badly. "Don't I?" I asked.

She surprised me by leaning gently forward and brushing her lips quickly against mine. Then she pulled away and stood up. "Of course," she said. "And you're right. Everything is going to be just fine." We floated in an awkward silence for a moment, then Annemarie said, "I'm going to bed," and headed for her room.

"Hey," I said. "You still didn't tell me where you went today."

She didn't answer, just kept going. I watched her, and found myself in the odd position of wishing Annemarie would come back and convince me she was right, that everything, indeed, was going to be a-okay.

# Chapter 8

# New Beginnings

ANNEMARIE

Richard had skipped town. Family emergency, they said at the office. I tried to believe it.

Something happened to his mother. She did have high blood pressure. Or his father, who suffered from rheumatoid arthritis. God forbid one of his siblings. God forbid! We had a wedding to pull off in a couple of months.

I don't know what Lilah thought when I rushed out of the kitchen that morning on the pretence of having to get to work, but I didn't care. I needed information as quickly as possible, and if it came, I wanted to process it in privacy, so I left Lilah and headed for my office. I dropped my bag and checked my phone to see whether there was a message from Richard. There wasn't. My heart sank. Nor was there one from Zachary Link. My heart sank harder.

Mr. Link was checking out this morning, I knew, and I wanted to touch base before he left, to smooth things over after our last awkward exchange. As for Richard, he would surely call later, and I would help him through whatever he was going through. I slipped out of my office, into the elevator, up to the top floor and Zachary Link's suite.

My heart was beating hard and fast as I walked briskly down the hall. *You're moving too fast,* I told myself. *Better slow down — you don't want to be panting when Zachary Link answers the door. If he answers the door.*

There was every chance he'd left hours ago to catch an early flight. As my sandals padded softly against the hall carpet, I convinced myself that if he had indeed left, I wouldn't care. I stared into the numbers on the door—502—and rapped my knuckles against the wood gently. When I heard movement inside the room, I felt a strange, exhilarating thrill.

He opened the door and looked at me, and for a moment, I thought I'd made a terrible mistake. I checked out his outfit. Today he wore straight leg jeans and a V-neck T-shirt, emerald with white and mint batik emblazoned on the chest, like a shield. The look on his clean-shaven face was hard to read—puzzled, annoyed, surprised? Then he smiled, his megawatt smile turning the full force of its charm on me, and I had to grab onto the door frame to steady myself. "Annemarie," he said. "Are you all right?"

I nodded. "It's been one of those mornings." Should I tell him that I nearly crumpled from ecstatic admiration of his beautiful face combined with relief that he was glad to see me? What could I do, now that my whole life was falling to pieces, the house I had so diligently and carefully built morphing into something completely unfamiliar? Maybe I didn't have a magic wand to fix all that immediately, but there was one thing I could do. Stay professional. Briskly, I said, "I just wanted to apologize for yesterday."

He stepped back from the door, making a clear path for me to enter. His luggage—one suitcase and a carry-on—was packed and waiting, sitting by the large king-size bed, its amber satin sheets disheveled from his sleep. He walked by me and sat near the picture window at the cherry wood table with the remains of English Breakfast tea and Lilah's delectable cherry scones on it. Motioning to the chair across from him, he said, "Please."

I relaxed into the seat, suddenly feeling how unbelievably exhausted I was. "Aren't you leaving?" I asked.

"After lunch," he said. "I have a late afternoon flight."

"Back to California."

"Yes," he said. "I thought I'd order a picnic and drive my rental car west of the city."

"Oh?"

"Mmmm." His voice sounded smooth and rich and delicious, like freshly whipped cream. "There's a state park where I like to hike. Last time I visited, I found the most wonderful mossy glade." He smiled at me again. "Would you like to come?"

Come? I had to work, and I didn't even know what a mossy glade was. I thought of Richard, toying with me, leaving me in the lurch, and I knew instantly I would go. I looked at my watch, tapping it lightly with one finger, making a pretense of thinking about it. "Well," I said. "It's possible."

"On one condition." I looked up, flustered. A demand? "You must finally agree to call me Zach."

I laughed, and surprised myself with the loud, ringing sound of my own voice. "I have to take care of a few things. Can I meet you somewhere in half an hour?"

We arranged to rendezvous at the coffee shop on the corner by the hotel. I rushed to the office to check messages again—still no Richard, which was almost a relief under the current circumstances. I told Carol I had an emergency and I'd see her tomorrow, rushed home, and changed into khaki shorts, a white tank top, and sneakers. Within the hour I was sitting next to Zachary Link in the front seat of a rented Lexus, speeding into suburbs I'd never before explored.

"I like taking these back roads," he said. "You get to see things like this." Zach—I was getting used to calling him that—pointed to a body of water, tall, dark, craggy trees sprouting from it like giant bogey men. Suddenly, a long-necked bird alighted from one and burst into spectacular flight, its wing span massive and graceful.

"Oh my," I gasped. "That's beautiful."

"It's a nesting spot for blue herons," said Zach.

I had never seen such a thing before. The only birds I ever noticed were the pigeons that swarmed all over the city. I kept my eyes on the heron until it was a speck, until we were back to rolling green hills, another sight I didn't often see. Zach started humming. I didn't recognize the tune. "What's that?" I asked.

"It's called 'Wild Woman'," he said, then added with a smile, "Don't tell me you've never heard it."

It was familiar, but I just couldn't place it. "I might have," I said, puzzling.

"It's a big Eats hit right now." The realization hit me like a brick. Of course I knew it. Richard loved the song. Zach brushed my forearm quickly and gently, saying, "It could be about you." I thought my heart was going to burst from the confusion. Richard had said the exact same thing more than once, even singing segments of the song in my ear. Meanwhile, Zach's fingers tickling my arm reminded me of Lilah's feather and the way Richard had used it on me just the day before.

"You okay?" Zach asked.

"Of course," I answered. "Why do you ask?"

"You look a little flushed." His smile held more amusement than concern, but that was fine. To my surprise, I was starting to feel relaxed. It was as though leaving the scheduled, bustling grind of the city allowed me to worry less about making sure everything happened in a particular way.

Or maybe it had something to do with the other night's sex session with Richard. It had been in the back of my mind ever since it happened. We had done things I thought I would never allow in bed, and yet the thrill I felt each time I thought of them — the feel of the scarves holding me fast, Lilah's vibrator, the sight of Richard's erection smushed between my breasts — well, the thrill was palpable. It sizzled between my legs, tingled and warmed my belly, and caught my breath. I even enjoyed the tiny kernel of shame that welled up. Instead of making me shrink inside, it felt conspiratorial and good. Suddenly I remembered the line that Richard sang into my ear: *Wild woman/I know you are in there/come out and play dirty/ I need you to take that dare.* Had he just wished, or had he known? And why in heaven's name did he leave just as it was beginning to happen?

"Annemarie." Zach's voice broke my reverie, and I happily came back to the present.

"Wow," I said. "This is fantastic." Zach pulled the Lexus off the road, and drove through a wooded setting on a dirt path.

He parked in an unpaved lot, and we both got out of the car. "Come on," he said, holding out the hand without the picnic basket.

I took it, reveling in its size and strength, the way it gripped my own with surety yet softness. I couldn't help but compare it to Richard's whose hand was more urgent and more yielding to me. The comparisons didn't detract from either man. I found them both wonderful.

We walked in silence for a few minutes. There were wildflowers on the path, curved pink blossoms rounded as though taking a bow and tiny blooms of bright yellow that reminded me of twinkling starlight. Nothing was more prominent than the green, lush and growing all around us on the ground, on bushes, and on trees, all manner and shapes and sizes of leaves and grass and weeds. It shaded and cooled us as we walked, creating a magical interplay of light and shadow that made me feel like I was in a storybook.

And wasn't I? Wasn't I with an important, rich man who also happened to look like a movie star, and who obviously wanted me very badly? The complicating facts—like his marriage and my crumbling engagement—well, didn't I deserve to just forget about those for an afternoon, and if I did forget about them, didn't Richard deserve it for what he was putting me through?

"Here we are," Zach whispered, his voice like honeyed silk in my ear. The spot was gorgeous. It was as though the wood had opened its mouth and blown out an airy, perfect space. The clearing was cozy, big enough for two yet shielded by the comfort of trees. I breathed deeply, and felt like I understood for the first time the meaning of the phrase fresh air.

The most amazing thing was the ground, laid out with fuzzy green. It covered the area like a carpet. As I knelt down to touch it I realized it was softer and cooler than any rug could ever be. "This is moss," I said out loud in my wonderment. I was petting the ground as though it were a cat.

Zach laughed. "You've never touched moss before?"

I shook my head. Zach knelt beside me, putting two fingers under my chin and slowly turning me to face him. "Now I get to touch something new." He caressed my cheeks, making circles that sent chills through me, and traced the outline of my lips with one finger.

Almost involuntarily, my mouth opened and I met his fingertip with my tongue, pulling his finger in and gently biting it. Then my eye caught the ring on the finger of his left hand, and I pulled back, horrified. "What is it?" he said.

I pointed to the ring. "Do you have to wear that?"

"Yes," he said, with utmost seriousness. "I do."

"It's kind of distracting."

"No more than that rock on your lovely finger," he said, gesturing to my diamond.

I turned away and felt tears welling up. What a mess I was in. I, Annemarie Fitch, who had never been anything but put together, successful, and in charge, was in a pickle. A huge one. In fact, a whopper.

Zach wiped the tear running down my cheek with such tenderness that it made me cry harder. "Do you want to talk about it?" he asked.

"No," I said. "What I want to know is what the hell you're doing here with me."

"Having lunch," he said, pulling a brightly-colored oil cloth from the basket and spreading it out before us. "I hope you're hungry."

"You're avoiding the question," I said.

"Not in the least," he answered, setting a bottle of champagne, two glasses, a hunk of cheese, a baguette, and some grapes onto the cloth.

"Then answer me," I said. All the good feelings of a few moments ago had slipped away. Instead I felt raw and shaky and scared.

He popped the cork and poured a glass of champagne for each of us, handed me one, and said, "I want to get to know you."

"Why?" I asked, taking a bubbly swallow. "Oh god, that's good." It was about the best champagne I'd ever had.

He laughed. "Now try this." He slathered a hunk of bread with creamy brie. I ate, nodding my head in appreciation. "I'd like to tell you about my marriage," said Zach.

The last thing I wanted was to listen to how unhappy he was, how he and his wife couldn't relate to each other, what a burden her special dietary needs were, and how he was about to ask for a separation. Nor did I want to unload about the disaster I was living. "Zach, I don't want to hear about your troubles. They don't matter. Let's just have a good time, okay?" He looked astonished for a moment, then laughed so hard he nearly spilled his champagne. "What's so funny?" I asked.

"You surprise me, Annemarie. Continually. In pleasant ways."

"So," I said, snuggling closer to where he was sitting on the moss. "We're on the same page."

He sidled up next to me. The feel of his muscled arm against mine, and the anticipation of what we could do on that exquisite moss, turned me on quite a lot. "Not exactly," he said.

"What?"

"My marriage is great. I love my wife, and we're very happy together."

This caught my interest. "Do tell," I said, getting myself more bread and cheese.

"We're polyamorous."

"What's that?" I asked. I had some idea of what it was. I knew, for instance, that it was something like what Lilah had with her multiple partners. In fact, she had used that word about herself more than once, but I wanted to hear Zach's interpretation.

"It means that we're committed to each other in our primary relationship, but that we recognize each other's freedom to explore relationships with others."

"Wait a minute," I said. "I need another glass of champagne." Once he had poured for me, I settled on the moss and put my head on his shoulder. "So let me get my brain around this. You and your wife give each other permission to have sex with other people?"

"It's not just sex," he said. "Or it might be. Actually, Joanne's more likely to have a one-night stand than I am."

"Joanne. That's your wife."

"Yes," he said, popping a red grape into my mouth. "I tend to want relationships that are more lasting."

"Really," I laughed. "And how many girlfriends do you keep on the side?"

I thought I saw a look of pain cross his face, but it was fleeting. "None, at the moment. I had one, but she broke up with me to get married."

"Why'd she have to break up with you," I whispered. "If your wife didn't care."

"The man she married wanted to be monogamous." He looked sad again. "I wanted to be friends, but she said she couldn't risk her marriage."

I looked far into his blue eyes, and got an inkling of how deep a person could go with him. "I'm not a shrink or anything," I said. "But aren't you just getting yourself into the same situation all over again?"

He met my gaze, and I practically melted when he said, "I hope not."

"Zach," I said, reaching for his beautiful hair and running the ringlets through my fingers. "How is it that you have an interest in me? You know nothing about me, and all I've ever done is wait on you."

"Well," he said, "I know you're stunningly beautiful." He undid the clasp that held my hair back, and my long locks fell out in a swirl on my shoulders. He had more to say, but I understood that he wanted to wait a moment, and I let him worship my hair with his hands, then pay homage to my neck. He ran his finger down it, toward the edge of my tank top, teasing the spot just above my cleavage, where Richard's sex had pulsed warm, wet cream so recently.

"Zach," I whispered, moving his hand lower, to my breast, where my nipple hardened through the cotton fabric of my shirt.

He pulled his hand away and fed me another grape. "You're right," he said. "I don't know you. But I sense you, and what I sense, I like."

"What do you sense?"

"That you're bright, intelligent, exciting, and adventurous."

"That's funny," I said. "That last thing. I don't think you're right about that."

Zach stretched out on the bed of moss so he was lying on his back, looking into the sky. "I beg to differ," he said. "You're here, aren't you? And you didn't hesitate in coming for a minute."

He was right. I had done that. I lay beside him on my back, and we stayed quiet for awhile, side by side, watching the sky together.

Shortly after one o'clock Zach said, "I should get back if I don't want to miss my plane."

"Do you have to work tomorrow?" I asked. We were lying intertwined now, the soft moss cushioning my side, my front pressed against Zach, my leg wrapped around his hip.

"No," he said.

"Then miss the plane," I answered. After all, we hadn't even kissed yet. We'd spent the better part of an hour and half talking.

"Sweet Annemarie," he said. His mouth was so close to mine that our noses touched, and I could feel his calm, warm breath. We looked at each other, and our faces moved slowly toward one another like compasses seeking north. Neither Zach, nor I, initiated that first kiss, but it happened.

The moment our mouths met and I felt Zachary Link's full, generous lips envelop mine, I knew I was changed. As we slowly opened the kiss wider, made it wetter, warmer, more urgent, I felt flooded with an intense relief. When our tongues found each other, swimming hungrily to greater depths, I felt freer than I had ever been.

Did I forget to mention hornier than I'd ever been? Zach wanted it, too, I could feel the hardness pressing against my khaki shorts, but where I'd thrown caution and control to the wind, he was still very much in charge of his life. "Annemarie," he whispered. "We'll see each other again soon."

"Don't go," I said, biting his earlobe and holding him tight against me as he tried to get up.

He laughed. "I knew you were a wild woman." He put his hands on my shoulders and gently pushed me away. I relented.

"When?" I asked. "When will I see you?"

"I'll come back in a few days," he said. "I promise." I helped him pack up the picnic and we walked back to the car hand in hand, and remained quiet for most of the ride home.

He dropped me off at my apartment building. "One last kiss," he whispered, leaning toward me and planting his gorgeous lips on mine. It was a long one, and as I let myself in the front door, I felt warmer than I had in a long time.

I also felt intrigued. Zach had talked a little about Joanne. Apparently she knew about me—Zach had told her of his attraction the first time he laid eyes on me. He was on a business trip and had dined at the hotel. He'd seen me in the lobby working with an elderly, very rich guest in a wheelchair. After making inquiries, he found out I worked at the hotel and booked it for his next trip. He had been wondering how to make contact with me and was pleasantly surprised when I came to his door.

Zach asked about Richard, and I told him there wasn't much to tell. We were deliriously happy until yesterday, when he disappeared. "How do you know something is wrong?" he asked. "It's only been a day." I almost bought the story myself, then Zach mentioned something about trusting my intuition, and I burst into tears.

On the elevator up to the apartment, I put my hair into a bun and straightened my clothes out as best I could. What would I face once inside? A message from Richard? A letter saying it was over? Maybe even Richard himself?

None of the above. Just Lilah, looking guilty. I met her in the hall, as I was taking off my sneakers. "Li," I said.

"Hey," she answered. I wanted to check the phone machine, but something told me to stay and talk to Lilah first. After she confessed her meeting with Richard, who was apparently struggling but still wanted to marry me, I went into my room and shut the door. So Richard was confused. How could I hold that against him, after today? After today, I was confused, too. I thought I still wanted to marry Richard, but I had no idea what I wanted our marriage to be like. Then I thought about how it was all Richard's fault. Only the day before I'd had none of these doubts and fears and, damn it, vulnerabilities, and I felt myself get angry.

It was no use, though, being mad. Everything had changed, and maybe Richard was just brave enough to want to change the terms of our marriage before we tied the knot instead of after. But hadn't we agreed on terms already? If we had, I realized, they had been my terms. I thought Richard was happy to go along with them, but maybe I'd been ignoring him, being cowardly and selfish. And now, after Zach, my terms didn't make sense even to me.

Zach. What would become of us? I had no idea, but the warm feeling of sweetness inside me said it would be something good. I stripped off my clothes and ran my hands along my own body, making goose bumps on my skin. I gently pinched my nipples, still firm with arousal. With as light a touch as I could muster, I tapped on my clitoris, swollen with thoughts of Zach. Then I saw that Lilah's feather and vibrator were still on my bed, and that made me think of Richard and the last time we had sex, which made me even wetter.

I lay on my bed, still unmade from the other night, messy with mine and Richard's lovemaking. With my legs spread wide, I used the soft tip of the feather to tickle my sex, which ached with wanting. No more waiting, not another moment. I thrust the vibrator inside me as deeply as I could and flicked one of the two switches on the remote control. The purple rod began to twirl around inside me, massaging the walls of my vagina. I turned the other switch, and the whole thing began to buzz. I pressed it to me so the rabbit ears were vibrating against my clitoris. I came immediately.

I left the vibrator inside me and looked at my wet, satiated sex, the lips swollen and pink and happy. The sensuousness of it overwhelmed me—Richard making me surrender to him, Zachary Link's deep eyes and tender kiss, the woods, the sky, the moss. My life was falling apart, and yet new doors were opening, new doors that beckoned untold pleasure.

Or was it pain? I thought of Zach's sadness at the loss of a woman he loved. Maybe those doors only promised ruin and pain.

I pressed the remote accidentally and Lilah's vibrator started to gyrate inside me, and I found I was wet again. I put all thoughts aside, and let myself be taken away by another orgasm, then fell into sleep.

# Chapter 9
# The Night I Saw Richard

**LILAH**

I was in a state like I hadn't been in for years, not since I was eighteen and forlorn and teary-eyed over a boy. What was wrong with me? Nothing terrible happened. I was about to get Chad in the sack—probably. Jenn had a delicious new lover that she was willing to share with me again—hopefully. Richard intended to change the rules in his relationship with Annemarie, which could mean something tasty for me—maybe. All these things boded well for yummy things coming my way in the near future, so why did I feel so out of whack?

True, my closest friends were acting strangely. So what? I'd been through that before. People are weird. You let them do their thing and stand by or help out, depending on the situation. It always passed. So I told myself that *my* thing, whatever it was, would pass, too.

The pressing question was, what would I do with myself for two whole days off until Thursday when Chad was on the schedule? I could call him, but that didn't feel exactly right. I was essentially his boss, after all. The whole work thing would have to get worked out somehow, but I knew it was doable. Jenn and I managed it just fine.

Besides, two days off was a blessing. Normally, I'd be thrilled with the time. If I felt like being alone, I'd do yoga, go to a movie, treat myself to dinner out, or spend a delicious evening with my toys. If I felt like painting the town, I'd call Jenn, or one of my more occasional lovers. But I didn't want to do any of that. Horror of horrors, I didn't know what I wanted to do. That was most decidedly unlike me.

*Wait it out*, I told myself. *Meditate. Maybe something will come along.*

Late Tuesday morning, while I was in the middle of painting my toe-nails red, it did. My cell buzzed bright and early—Annemarie. *Call me* appeared on my screen. I thought about not doing it, but a stab of guilt quickly squashed that idea. I dialed her number and braced myself for the onslaught of tears.

"Hey, sweetie." *What? She sounded happy.*

"Hi," I said.

"Boy, do I have a surprise for you."

"Oh?" I immediately thought of Richard, and my heart thumped a little.

"Who's playing at the Capitol tomorrow?" Of course I knew. It was The Eats. I loved The Eats, but I hadn't gotten tickets in time. Jenn had managed to get one, but I wasn't willing to pay the kind of money she had forked over. "Lilah," Annemarie sang repeatedly, sounding like she was doing a rendition of "Tiptoe Through the Tulips."

"What?" I snapped.

"It's The Eats. Your favorite."

"I know." My hand slipped and shiny red polish smeared the top of my foot. "Damn!"

"I have two tickets for you." I was so busy wiping the color off my skin that I didn't absorb what she was saying. "Did you hear me, Li?"

"Yeah," I said absently. "Two tickets." As I was dabbing my foot with nail polish remover her words began to penetrate, but of course I didn't believe them. This must be payback, Annemarie's idea of a joke. "You're kidding, right?"

"No." She sounded absolutely giddy. "Not only that, I have a back-stage pass."

"Why are you doing this to me?" My foot clean, I was back to polish-ing, which was no easy task given the agitation that was beginning to race through my blood.

"You love them, don't you?" I said nothing. "Don't you?"

"You know I do, but they've been sold out for weeks."

"I know," she answered. "I have connections."

If anyone had connections, it would be Annemarie. Maybe, just may-be, this was for real. I finished up my pinky toe and closed the bottle. "How?" I asked, beginning to believe her, and beginning to sound as glee-ful as she did.

"Just call it an employee perk."

I remembered last week's talent convention, and figured the tickets had something to do with that. She must have buttered up some big wig, but why go after something she didn't want? "You don't like The Eats," I said.

"That's why I'm giving them to you."

"Are you serious?"

"I am, Lilah."

That was it. Annemarie would never take a joke this far. Talk about wiping out the doldrums with one blow. I was on top of the world. "Honey, you are the best."

"I know," she said. "And don't you forget it. They're holding the tickets under your name at the box office. Have fun."

We hung up and I jumped out of my chair. I wanted to dance around the kitchen, but I was afraid I'd mess up my toenails. Who to bring, that was the next question. Jenn was already going. Chad? Nah. I was still mulling over what to do about him, but The Eats didn't seem right. That's when the idea hit me. I should have rejected it on principle, immediately, instantly, and unequivocally.

Instead I picked up my cell and started to text Richard, then thought better of it and decided to call him. "Hello," he said.

"Hey, Ricky."

"Lilah?" He sounded disappointed.

"Yes," I said. "Who else would it be?"

"I thought it might be Annemarie using your phone."

I ignored that. "What are you doing tomorrow tonight?"

"Nothing important," he answered. "I mean, I have a date but I can always cancel."

"A date?" Funny how my back got up right away, and not necessarily for Annemarie's sake.

"I'm kidding," he said. "I'm doing nada. Just sitting around, trying to figure out my life."

"Not anymore," I cried. "You're coming to see The Eats with me!" Silence on the other end. "Did you hear me?"

"Yeah, I heard you," Richard said, sounding unconvinced. "I'm not sure if I believe you."

"You know you want to go." He'd told me months ago that he'd tried to convince Annemarie to go with him, but she wouldn't. I told him I'd take her place, but he ignored me. I knew then that things weren't as perfect in Annemarie's relationship as she made them out to be. And hadn't I been circling ever since, like a vulture waiting for the opportune moment? And didn't the opportune moment just present itself, ironically enough, from Annemarie herself?

"Where'd you get them?" he asked.

Richard knew about my failure to purchase in time, and my subsequent refusal to seek out overpriced resale tickets to a sold out show. I faltered, but only for a moment. "A friend," I said. It wasn't a lie.

He was quiet for a minute, probably wondering whether he should do it. Then he said, in a conspiratorial tone that thrilled me, "How are we getting there?"

"Let's cab it," I said. "Then we don't have to worry about parking."

We planned to meet for dinner then head to the concert. I suggested Patty Pete's again, for safety's sake, but Richard said he'd rather go to Chef Wong's. I agreed without asking questions, even though my antenna told me something was going on if Richard wanted to meet me at his and Annemarie's regular haunt.

Whatever. I was too excited to care.

On Wednesday night I dressed carefully, choosing comfortable clothes appropriate for the summer night and a packed concert. I wanted them to be sexy, too, as sexy as I'd been feeling for the last couple of days, and given the special occasion, just a little flashy.

A tight white camisole made of stretch cotton, with little silver studs beaded along the deep scoop neck, and a black cotton skort that showed off my legs. A few key pieces of jewelry, including a snaky arm bracelet, a silver toe ring, and a red ruby stud in my nose, and I was set. I ran a shimmery red gloss over my lips, the only make-up I ever wore, to match the toenails.

When I got to Chef Wong's, Richard was already there. "This place is empty," I said. "Not a good sign."

"It's early, and it's Wednesday."

"Whatever," I said. I had gone there once on a date with Patrick, the old bartender from Rialto's, and I'd forgotten how hideous the place was. Red wallpaper textured with a fuzzy gold pattern covered the walls. The fuzz was wearing off in places, making it look extra tacky. The indoor/outdoor carpeting was the ugliest mustard yellow color I'd ever seen. Statues of gilded lions and grinning Buddhas were all over the place. I put down my menu without looking at it. "I'll just have a bowl of white rice," I said.

"Come on," said Richard. "Try the Lo Mein. That's what Annemarie always gets."

I bristled at the speaking of her name. "No thanks," I said. "I can't believe Annemarie actually comes here."

Richard smiled and got a faraway look in his dark eyes. They glowed with a soft fire, and a slight flush bloomed on his sculpted cheeks. "We came here on our first date," he said. "She's a sentimental kind of girl." He was obviously madly in love with her, nothing I didn't already know, but he was so much more my kind of guy, someone who could love and worship and still want—no, need—to be free to explore all of his nature.

We ordered our white rice and General Gao's chicken and were served tea. I sipped the bitter liquid and smiled at Richard. It was great to see him without perfectly coiffed hair, a clean-shaven face, and those preppy clothes he always wore to work. I loved how he'd let his curls go, falling loose and soft around his head. His recent lack of attention to shaving gave him a rugged, edgy look. The white V-neck he wore showed off his thick neck and ample biceps nicely. All in all, the look suited the real Richard, at least what I thought was the real Richard, much more than his workaday image. But still, he had chosen this place which belonged to that Richard, the one that courted and won Annemarie Fitch, prize of prizes among women. I clutched a few grains of rice between my chopsticks and said, "Why are we here, Richard?"

He was clearly enjoying his chicken. "To eat," he said. "Before The Eats." He laughed at his own joke, which wasn't very good. Richard's jokes never were.

"Why here?" I said. "Were you hoping to run into Annemarie?"

"On the contrary," he answered. "She'd never come here without me."

His arrogance surprised me. I thought he was dead wrong. I thought Annemarie would come by herself to pine—if she were acting normal, that is. Suddenly I felt a flare of anger. "You haven't even asked how she's doing."

He stared at me hard. "How is she doing, Lilah?"

His look shamed me. Was I that transparent? Of course I was. I couldn't hide a damn thing. For a fleeting moment I wondered whether that was why I made sure there was never anything significant to reveal, but I wasn't about to dwell on that. "Actually," I whispered, holding his gaze. "She's doing remarkably well."

All the hardness left him, and he looked scared and vulnerable. "I know," he said. "I talked to her."

"You called her?" Now it was my turn to be surprised.

"Yes," he said.

"Well, that's great," I said. "You should have done it a long time ago."

He put down his fork and looked imploringly at me. Geez, he was all over the map. "Lilah, help me understand what's going on."

"What did she say?"

"First she yelled at me and called me a selfish prick bastard."

I laughed. "Good for her."

"That I could take. It's what came after that I don't get." I sat silently, waiting, letting him take the time he needed. "She asked if I just wanted a last fling, and I said not exactly." He stopped talking for a minute, as if to collect himself. I put my hand on his and squeezed it. "She said now that I changed all the rules, things were different for her, too. She was crying, but she sounded— different. I don't know what it means." He looked at me. "What does it mean?"

"I have no idea," I said.

"You're her best friend. She must be talking to you."

"Richard, I know you hoped I would be your go-between, but I never agreed to that."

"Tell me what's going on."

"I wouldn't if I knew, which I don't," I said. "Annemarie is the one you should be talking to."

"Damn you," he said, pulling his hand away. "You know and you won't help me."

"No, Richard," I said. "I'm as confused as you are. I agree she's acting weird. Almost happy. I don't understand it."

"Neither do I," he said, shaking his head. "Lilah, she asked if I wanted to be with other women."

"What did you say?"

"I told her I wanted to explain it to her, what it means, that it doesn't mean I don't love her."

"How did she take it?"

"She said she thought she understood."

"What?" Something very weird was going on, something Annemarie was keeping entirely to herself.

"She said she thought we should spend a couple of weeks apart, do some soul searching, then get together and talk."

"A couple of weeks," I said, frantically calculating dates in my head. "That would leave a little more than a month before the wedding."

He nodded. "If there is a wedding."

We both sat in silence, staring at our food. I felt a little shell shocked. *Come on, Lilah,* I told myself. *Play your role. Be the comforter.* "There will be," I whispered. "Of course there will be." I took his hand, his big, strong, hand, and to my delight, he began to stroke my palm with his thumb.

I stroked him back and could feel the current between us. Would there or wouldn't there be a wedding? I didn't know, and with some effort, I convinced myself that at least temporarily, I didn't care. Tonight, there would be The Eats with a free Richard.

And, I told my wanton, wanting pussy, a very good night it was going to be.

# Chapter 10
# Eats Alive

**LILAH**

Nothing turned out according to plan, but the way things were going, why should that have surprised me?

Problem number one occurred upon entrance to the stadium when we immediately ran into Jenn, who looked positively delicious. She had chosen chartreuse, a color only she could pull off. Her mini-dress was skimpy but loose. Hanging on her thin frame, it looked no shapelier than it would on a hanger in a closet. But then it wouldn't have Jenn's elegant arms and legs accenting it, and her skin that looked and tasted like cream. On her sweet little hands she wore tight, shiny, apricot gloves that went all the way up to her elbow. Unlike me, Jenn was a make-up girl, and she had done a great job on her face with gold eye shadow and coral lips that were anything but innocent, but somehow Jenn looked like a doll, girlish and sexy. "Honey pot," she cried when she saw me, throwing her gloved arms around me.

"These are awesome," I said, rubbing the orange, clingy satin.

Richard liked them, too. "May I?" He reached out to stroke them before Jenn even had a chance to answer.

Judging from her smile and the twinkle in her eye, that was more than fine with her. "They feel nice, don't they?" she asked.

Oh, well. I'd hoped to have Richard for myself the first time, but it seemed as though sharing was in order. I didn't mind too much, given how enticing Jenn looked and how incredibly hot she'd been of late.

Hordes of people bouncing us around as they passed interrupted the flirting. "Where are you sitting?" Jenn yelled over the din. I showed her our tickets. "How'd you score these?"

"A friend," I said.

"I'm way up in the rafters," Jenn said, pouting.

Richard, ever the gentleman, said, "You're welcome to trade tickets with me."

Before I could figure out a good way to object, Jenn accepted the offer with a squeal. "Thank you," she cried, hugging him and planting a big one right on his lips, lingering there just a nanosecond too long.

We planned a meeting place in the lobby after the concert. I hadn't even told Richard about the backstage pass. I was feeling pretty torn about it. It was a great opportunity, obviously. Maybe even once in a lifetime. But the same could be said for the evening's potentialities with Richard.

Jenn and I fully enjoyed our amazing seats. We got unbelievable views of the band, including Prado, the lead singer. There he was in the flesh, without airbrushing or Photoshop, and he did not disappoint. The Eats had always been about sex—one of the reasons I liked them so much and probably one of the reasons Annemarie didn't. Their music was suggestive, to say the least, and so were their moves.

They were shirtless, and it looked like they all worked out, but none of them could match Prado whose biceps rivaled Richard's. He stroked and kissed the microphone like it was a sex object. Several times he lowered it to the level of his bulge, wonderfully apparent in his blue silk pants, and hip thrusted it.

The Eats had the music going on, too. It was an amazing concert, full of tight, driving tunes for throngs of hot, sweating, dancing people. I was in heaven. I loved The Eats, and I loved crowds and their primal nature. When it was over, Jenn and I were both so happy we hugged for a long time. As she pressed her body against mine, she moved her hips in a slight, barely perceptible way that told me she was as horny as I was. I couldn't help licking her ear and taking a little suck on her earlobe. She giggled and said, "Let's go find Richard."

He was at the designated post-concert meeting place, looking thrilled. He was saying something about the concert, but who could hear over all the noise, and besides, I had to take a wicked pee. As the three of us were being bandied about in the mass of people, I yelled that I'd be right back. Jenn was nodding her head emphatically so I was sure she understood.

I couldn't have been gone more than a couple of minutes, but when

I returned, they were nowhere to be found. The lobby was still packed, so I searched around for a little while to no avail. I felt like an abandoned kid, except instead of being scared, I was furious. How could they do this to me? I found the quietest corner I could and pulled out my cell. I texted both Jenn and Richard and got no response. I dialed Jenn's number, but according to her message, her mailbox was full. I dialed Richard, but he didn't answer. Damn them! I could just go to Jenn's place, or to Richard's — I could go looking for them, except that it seemed pretty clear they didn't want me around.

Well, I wasn't going to cry about it. I raked through my little purse until I found the backstage pass that I thought I wouldn't be using.

*Please let me meet Prado*, I prayed, to no one in particular. *Please let me fuck Prado.*

Know that expression, be careful what you wish for? At first, I wandered through the sweaty, loud crowd trying to figure out where the hell to go. A backstage pass isn't much good if you don't know where to find the backstage.

I pushed my way through the swarms of people and approached a security guard. "Hi," I yelled. The guard was gray-haired, his arms folded over his paunch, which made a nice perch. He looked at me with a straight face and said nothing, just chewed what could have been gum or tobacco. I decided to try his approach, and simply flashed my pass. He pointed to something, but damned if I could see what it was through the throngs of people.

I continued to work my way through the commotion in the direction the guard indicated, and soon I saw a set of doors flanked by more security guards. My heart thumped and I felt a surge of adrenaline. To hell with Richard and Jenn. Let them go fuck themselves. More fun than that was waiting for me.

The ease with which I passed into the land of the exclusive people was a thrill in and of itself. All I found after I stepped through the doors, however, was a maze of hallways. Where to go? I smoothed my skort and my tank top, then picked a path. The hallways were big, gray, and full of echoes. The tapping of my sandals reverberated with every step I took. I tiptoed, listening, letting my ears guide me. Eventually, I heard the sound of laughter and talking, and gravitated to it.

There were people in a room. The door was open. Dare I go inside? I stood near the entrance, planning my next move, which turned out to be decided for me. Prado stepped into the hallway. He was walking fast. Before he could stop himself, or I could move, he plowed into me. *Hell of a way to meet a rock star,* I thought, as his firm, sweaty body collided with mine. "I'm sorry," I cried, expecting to back away. But Prado had me by the arms, and kept his body pressed against me.

I didn't know whether to be scared or thrilled or embarrassed. In truth, I was a bit of all three. Prado's face was inches from mine, and he was smiling. "Hey," he said softly. "Who are you?"

"Lilah," I whispered, barely breathing.

"Lilah," he repeated. His voice was quiet and hypnotic. His dark eyes held mine in a steady gaze, like a snake charmer. "Welcome."

"Prado," a voice called. A woman's voice. It was drawing near.

When she stepped into view my first thought was: *she's a giant.* She was already ridiculously tall to start with, but her black, thigh-high, spike-heeled boots made her downright statuesque. "Hey," she drawled when she saw me. "Who's this?" Her clothes, what there were of them, were black leather. Her make-up was severe, all black eyeliner and lipstick, and a glance at her hands revealed Wolverine-like daggers — they were silver, even — where her fingernails should have been.

Prado let go of me. My arms where he touched me were radiating heat, and I realized he'd been squeezing. "Lilah, Sue."

"Hello," I stammered, reaching out my hand.

I expected a firm, perhaps even painful grip, but Sue's hand took mine with delicacy, the dagger nails turned discreetly — and safely — downward. I breathed a sigh of relief, grateful that she didn't seem to be as scary as she looked. "We're going back to the hotel. You coming?"

Prado sidled up beside me. He was still shirtless. Up close, his washboard stomach was even sexier. He'd changed into jeans and left them unbuttoned and unzipped, revealing his generous bulge, hidden underneath some kind of skimpy metallic underwear. I badly wanted a piece of him. "Sure," I said. Overcome with boldness, or stupidity, or whatever drives people to do crazy things, I said, "Can I catch a lift with you?"

Sue smiled. She had quite a mouth, big and gummy and toothy. Her rectangular choppers looked especially white, framed as they were by matte black lips. I could understand the attraction to black, really I could. I liked it, too, but Sue went beyond. She had jet black hair, straight and long with square cut bangs. Her eyes were adorned with copious amounts of charcoal liner and mascara. Her ebony leather top looked like a bra and showed ample cleavage, which I had to admit looked inviting. Raven-colored leather hot pants hugged her ample ass. Then there were the wristbands — black, of course, with silver studs — and a collar that looked scarily tight on her long neck, jangly chains streaming from it, clipped to various metal loops on her garments. I didn't consider myself a sheltered person, but in my hip, earthy crunchy, free thinking, yoga world, I rarely encountered people like Sue.

We departed through a back door which opened onto a main street, where a limousine waited. I worried that we'd be accosted by fans, but no one seemed to notice that Prado of The Eats was out and about. He'd put on a T-shirt. It was bright yellow, and said *Never mind The Bollocks, here's the Sex Pistols.* In her spiked boots, Sue was at least a head taller than he was, and both of them were considerably taller than me. I felt like a kid being led around by her parents.

The driver held the door and I waited to see who would get in first. Sue pushed Prado along, then me. The limousine was elegant, with soft leather seats that felt positively sinful against the backs of my thighs. Inside it smelled of stale cigarette and marijuana smoke mixed with a perfume that reminded me of jasmine. As we pulled away, Prado put a hand on my thigh, sliding his fingers between it and the leather seat and holding tight to my leg.

I saw Sue take notice, but all she did was smile and pet my hair. I settled into the cushions, letting my leg fall further into the palm of Prado's hand, lulled by Sue's gentle stroking of my locks. The comfortable ride ended all too soon. In what felt like a few minutes, we were parked in front of the hotel. My hotel.

As we walked in, I kept my head down and pretended to be looking in my purse. I didn't want to run into any other hotel employees, and certainly not Annemarie. Once in the elevator, I relaxed. Prado pushed number 17, which didn't surprise me. I imagined we'd be heading for the luxury suites. Annemarie saw these rooms all the time. I had only seen them once, after begging her to take me up and show me. It was quite against the rules, but I managed to convince her. It was early in our friendship. I had thought that maybe I'd seduce her up there, but she was way too uptight.

Prado slipped his card key into its slot and pushed open the door. Several people were already there. A bare ass faced me. It belonged to a woman leaning over one of the plush couches, sucking the cock of a man whom I recognized as the band's drummer.

Another naked woman was on the couch beside him, feeding him her tits. On the carpet, a couple was deep into a loud, slurpy 69. In the corner, a woman with bleached hair and nipple rings sat with her legs splayed while a middle-aged lady with big, droopy tits and graying hair serviced her with an extra-large pink dildo. Bowls filled with multi-colored condoms and dental dams were everywhere I looked. At the desk along the far wall, a long-haired guy sat playing computer games on a laptop. He was the only person in the room wearing clothes. Except us, I realized.

"Welcome to our nest, Lilah," Sue crooned, taking my hand and leading me to the bar. Thankfully, it was near the picture window, which offered a stunning view of the city. I was able to look out at it while Sue poured me a beer. "Here you go," she said, handing me a frosty mug.

Prado came up next to me, slipping his arm around my waist. "Is this cool with you?" he asked. "Or you wanna cut this scene?"

I took a big swig of the cold beer. I wasn't a drinker, but beer was my one indulgence, and this was very good beer. I looked around at the orgy. Was I cool with this? Honestly, I was jazzed but a bit freaked out. I had no idea how to answer Prado's question, but the beer calmed my nerves enough to make me realize that I was wet, not surprising given the activity in the room.

Prado was watching something with rapt attention. I turned my head and saw that the 69 couple had changed things around. Now that his face wasn't buried in pussy, I recognized the lead guitarist. He was fucking the woman hard from behind, her tits jiggling as he rammed her. Prado's arm pulled me closer. "Mmm," he groaned. The growl sounded uninhibited and primitive, and very appreciative.

I think I nodded in agreement. Whatever I did, Prado took it as an affirmative, which he then took as encouragement to step away from me and disrobe. His cock was hard and enormous. Sue gave it an affectionate squeeze, with a little pinch at the tip. "Yeah, baby," she said. She looked at me, smiling. "Nice, huh?"

Before I knew it, a woman was on her knees in front of Prado, expertly sucking his cock. He held her head and fucked her mouth, his hips undulating like they did on stage. Another woman lay on the floor positioning herself under the kneeling woman's pussy, the better to eat her. I stared, dumbfounded and salivating. Sue jerked me out of my reverie by wrapping two fingers around one of my erect nipples. "Come on, girl," she said. "Go get some."

I looked down as her hand pulled away from my breast, the silver, sexy daggers brushing against me. In no time I was naked, too, but I didn't know how to join in. It looked like everyone in the room was taken. Not to worry. As soon as Prado saw me unclothed he looked at Sue, who nodded. At that signal, he pushed away the woman who was sucking him and reached for me.

He kissed me first, a surprising gesture in this mass of pure, hardcore sex. His tongue was skilled and energetic and probing, yet gentle. It left my mouth and licked my earlobes, my neck, making a trail down my body, between my breasts, along my belly. At my pussy, he stopped, grabbing a condom and sliding it on, and tearing open a square of latex from a bowl on the floor. He placed it on my mound, lapping there, first one side then the other, all around my clit but not touching it. I spread my legs so he could get at it and at my swollen lips. He continued to torture me, licking my mound and leaving the more sensitive parts longing.

I grabbed onto his long hair and tried to push him to the right place to no avail. Sue laughed out loud. She was still fully dressed, languidly smoking a cigarette and watching as though she were witnessing nothing out of the ordinary.

Prado looked at her again. Again she nodded. If I hadn't been so out of my mind horny I might have been taking note of their little exchanges and surmising what they might mean. As it was, all I wanted was for Prado to suck my clit, so I was glad to see the nod, and ecstatic when Prado finally stuck his sweet tongue into my slit. I came immediately, squeezing and pulling his hair, pushing my pussy hard into his face.

Before I knew what was happening, he scooped me into his arms, lifting me by the butt and forcing my legs around him. His buff muscles came in handy for that move. He was a god, I decided as he guided his dick inside me. With adeptness and admirable control, he created a perfect fucking rhythm, convincing me that if he wanted to, he could lift up the entire world, like Atlas. I realized I could let myself go limp in his arms, and I did. My legs spread wider and my ass sunk lower, freeing Prado's mammoth cock to slide in deeper.

I let myself utterly relax, the only tension in my body in the arms which were wrapped around Prado's neck, hugging his broad shoulders for support. Sue knelt down beside us to get a better view of Prado's cock pumping me. She tickled my exposed anus with one of her long fingernails, teasing it. I remembered the feel of Iona's finger, and I wished that Sue would penetrate me that way.

Suddenly, Prado put me down and grabbed my hand. Sue followed as we stepped over kneeling, lying, sitting, tangled-up bodies, through a door into an empty bedroom. Sue turned the lock behind us.

The three of us were alone, Prado and I naked, panting, and covered with sweat and sex juice. Sue, on the other hand, was just as she had been when she first stepped into the hallway after my fateful meeting with Prado. Not for long, I realized as she began to unhook the front of her bodice. Her tits tumbled out. They were huge. I stared back and forth between them and Prado's large cock and realized what an exceptional couple they were.

Sue's tits weren't just gigantic. They were gorgeous, the most beautiful pair of knockers I'd ever seen. For all her obsession with darkness, her skin was as pale and smooth as porcelain, her nipples puckered and pink. They were also pierced, I realized as she unclasped one of the silver chains that hung from her collar and threaded the point through one nipple. She left the other nipple bare. "Come here, Lilah," she said in a controlled, soft voice I wouldn't have thought of disobeying.

I stepped forward and found that my head was right at the level of those glorious breasts. "Mama needs a good sucking," she said, lifting her tits toward my mouth. "Get to work, baby." I went first for the pierced nipple, drawing it in and enjoying the metallic taste mixed with Sue's heady aroma. It was definitely she who smelled so fine, like some exotic flower I couldn't quite identify. Whatever the scent, it was definitely an aphrodisiac. I buried my face in her cleavage, nursing one breast then the other until Sue said, "Enough."

She proceeded to get totally naked, except for the collar and wristbands and the chains that emanated from them. Her pussy was unshaven, and boasted a thick, curly bush that spread all the way to her legs. "That was very nice," she said to me. "But it doesn't change what a bad girl you are." Despite the punitive words, her voice was like silk, like the purring of a cat. "Mama and Daddy are going to have to punish you."

I looked at Prado. He laughed, throwing up his hands in an *oh well* kind of gesture, looking nothing like a daddy. "Fortunately," said Sue, pointing, "we have this little swing to help us." I turned and saw a strange contraption hanging from the ceiling.

"Get in," said Sue, lifting a wooden paddle from the table. What did I think of this? I had no idea. My pussy was hot again from the warmth and softness of Sue's cleavage and the sight of Prado's still erect cock. That was the only message I could hear at the moment. And wasn't I, Lilah, game for anything? Wasn't I?

The swing was hanging on some kind of spring, which allowed Prado to pull it down in order for me to climb in. There were two holes cut into thick black canvas, with a giant opening between them. I knew that big slit was to expose my pussy while I hung helplessly. The thought was excruciatingly exciting. I stepped into the holes, expecting Prado to let go and let me spring into the air. First Sue opened a night table drawer and pulled out a long piece of black fabric. I had just enough time to catch sight of a double headed black dildo before she blindfolded me.

That's when the fun began.

# Chapter 11

# Anticipation

**ANNEMARIE**

I felt like a teenager again, waiting for the weekend. Zach said he'd be back to see me, and the anticipation was blissful. As much as I wished that was all I could think about, in reality, a combination of things obsessed me.

Zach, and sex with him, were easy to think about, and in some ways felt like an escape from reality. Thoughts of Richard proved more difficult. I just couldn't sort that out in my head. The only thing I knew was that even though I still loved him, I was beginning to look at him differently. Not necessarily in a bad way, but in a way I didn't yet understand. Plus, I was mad at him. I knew well enough by now that my carefully constructed house would have come crashing down eventually, and the things we were working out now needed to be worked out, but I still didn't like it. I chose to handle the situation through avoidance. That was unlike me. Normally I'd beat that horse until I had full control of the situation.

I had another problem I'd never dealt with before. The sex thing had really taken over. My body was like a motor someone had flicked on, and I was revving. Four days felt like way too long for my engine to run without a few tune-ups. But what could I do? I wasn't about to call Richard, so I had to satisfy myself keeping company with Lilah's bunny and waiting for Zach.

At work, I let Carol handle more and more situations. She was thrilled with the added responsibility. She'd wanted to deal with top level guests for months, but I hadn't allowed it. As it turned out, she did a perfectly acceptable job and became a much nicer person. Had I been holding the reins too tightly? Had her bitchiness and long face been fueled by resent-ment directed at me? Whatever the answer, my carefully woven life was coming apart. Miraculously, I was letting go, and I crossed my fingers that it would all turn out right.

I got a jolt on Tuesday afternoon when Douglas called me into his office. I'd been late to work after oversleeping. If Richard's vanishing act had triggered the predictable trajectory, I'd be collecting professional ac-colades, drowning my troubles and squashing my fears at work. But my bed, and Lilah's vibrator, beckoned, and now I was in trouble.

"Douglas," I said, wearing my polished smile and offering my signa-ture handshake. I'd perfected it early in my career, mixing just the right amounts of firmness, friction, and release.

He stood behind his desk, leaning over to take my hand. "Annema-rie," he said. "A delight, as always." He gestured to the black leather chair, and I sat in it.

"What can I do for you, Douglas?" Whether he'd called me in for a disciplinary discussion or not, I had to be cool and confident.

He played with the fountain pen on his desk. His nails were mani-cured and buffed, his gray hair cut and styled perfectly. I admired his tie—simple peach silk and totally elegant. Douglas was a class act and a great boss. I had always respected his success and finesse, but I found myself looking at him with new eyes. As I stared at the gold band around his finger, I wondered about his wife. Christine was a lovely woman, ev-ery bit as refined as her husband. Until yesterday, I'd assumed everyone's marriage was the same. Now I understood that commitments can be as complex and unique as the individuals making them.

Douglas was looking down at his tie. He seemed almost embarrassed. His voice was soft when he spoke. "Are you all right, Annemarie?" I was taken aback. Douglas had never spoken to me like this before. "I know your wedding is coming up, but tardiness isn't like you."

I felt my face flush and imagined how ridiculously red I must look. "I'm sorry, Douglas. It won't happen again."

He turned to me. "Annemarie," he said with a laugh. "I'm not com-plaining. I'm concerned."

His kindness touched me. This was more than I expected and much more than I would have done for employees in my charge. "Thank you," I said, humbled.

Douglas smiled. "You're welcome. Let me know if there's anything you need or anything we can do."

I nodded, standing up. "I'm fine," I said, wringing my hands. "It's just wedding jitters, you know the drill."

On the way back to my office, I thought over what happened. Douglas and Carol, both acting in ways I'd never have expected, showing sides I didn't even know were there. What else had I been blind to?

I stepped out of the elevator and bumped into someone. "Excuse me, honey." The woman was wearing dark sunglasses with hot pink frames and coral lipstick that she actually carried off. She was familiar, but I couldn't place her.

"No problem," I said.

The woman smiled. "Annemarie," she said. "How are you?"

I concentrated. She could be someone important, and it was bad form to forget anyone, especially in a work situation. She pulled off her sunglasses, revealing sparkly blue eyes. I breathed a sigh of relief. "Jenn," I said. It was that little tart that worked with Lilah.

"Yeah," she said, giggling. "Where you headed?"

"My office," I answered.

She looked at me, her head tipped to the side. "Oh, work. Too bad." Her mouth shaped itself into something like a rosebud when she spoke.

"Was Lilah in today?" I really didn't need to be talking to her, but she was engaging. Adorable, actually.

"Mmmm," she answered, as though the idea of Lilah coming to work was delicious and sensuous. Lilah had told me about her relationship with Jenn—she called Jenn her fuck buddy. She might have been trying to propose that she and I engage in similar relations, but I never let her get that far in the conversation.

Jenn scrunched her button nose and giggled again. It dawned on me that she was flirting. For the second time in an hour, I felt myself blush. "Well," I said. "I have to go."

"Okay," said Jenn, slinging her batik bag over her shoulder. "See you later."

Back at my desk, I took my phone out of my bag and turned it back on. It had been off only for the short time I'd gone to see Douglas and already there were two messages and three texts. One call was from Zach. A rush of excitement went through me. The other call, as well as the texts, were from Richard, and that filled me with dread.

I should have been glad that Richard was reaching out, but I wasn't. It seemed that my entanglement with Zach was more important at the moment. I knew there was something wrong with that, but I'd started the ball rolling and now there was no stopping it. I decided to listen to Zach's message first. I didn't want my experience of it ruined by the wreck that was the rest of my life. "Annemarie," he said. I loved to hear him speak my name. "We should go somewhere together. Call me." A kiss blown into the phone, then, "Miss you."

Zach's message made my whole body feel warm and alive. I enjoyed it for a few minutes before I read Richard's frantic texts, and listened to his message. "Annemarie." He sounded terrified, which actually made me laugh. Wasn't he the one who initiated this? "I want to talk. Please call me." A pause, then an even more pathetic plea. "Please. I love you."

Normally, the whimpering would have made me very happy, but after squashing the tears his declaration of love almost elicited, I found it decidedly unattractive. Still, my heart went out to him. He was suffering, no doubt about it. I was, too. Both of us would be, until we worked everything through.

My desk phone rang, and I picked up. "Hey, Annemarie." It was Carol. "What's up?"

"Suite 2068 didn't like the massage therapist we sent him." That was Franklin Forcucci, construction company magnate in town to discuss a bid for a major urban reconstruction project. His dissatisfaction could only mean one thing. His definition of masseuse was prostitute, and that was something we didn't provide. I'd have to discreetly steer him in the right direction and let him make his own arrangements. "I'll take care of it," I said.

I spent the afternoon getting Mr. Forcucci off my back, arranging a menu for an in-suite cocktail party, and dealing with several special requests for incoming weekend guests. At 5:30, I was tired and famished, and planned to head home and grab some Thai food on the way.

As I gathered my belongings, my phone buzzed. Richard, again. I'd planned to call him once I was fed and comfortable at home, but since he'd rung me up again, I decided to get it over with. "Hello," I said.

"Annemarie." It came out in a rush of desperate breathlessness.

Suddenly, I wanted to cry again, which just wouldn't do. "Hi, Richard,"

I said, my voice tight and wavering.

"Are you okay?" I nodded, then realized he couldn't see me. "Annemarie?"

"Yes," I said. "I'm fine. And you?"

"I've been better," he said.

"Are you taking time off work?" I asked.

"Yes," he said.

"Did you lie to them, too?" He didn't answer. "Richard?"

"I miss you."

"But you're the one who left," I said. I was crying now, I couldn't help it. "Why didn't you just talk to me?"

"I didn't know how."

"You just open your mouth and say what you have to say." My voice was laced with sarcasm, and anger.

"It's not that easy," he said. "You don't make it easy."

"Don't blame me for your cowardice."

"I'm sorry. I tried to talk to you, lots of times. But you're right. It was my failure." He was silent. I could almost feel his agony.

"That doesn't matter now," I said. "Everything's different."

"How?" he asked.

"I don't know," I said. "It just is." Could I tell him about Zach? How could I explain such a thing? "Do you want to be with other women?" I asked.

He hesitated, but only for a moment. "It's not that simple," he said. I didn't answer. "What is it, Annemarie?"

"I think I understand."

"You do?" he said, sounding astonished.

I didn't know what to say, or how to say it. "Not yet," I said. "I'm not ready to talk."

"Can we plan a time?"

"Next week, maybe. Or the week after, actually. I need a couple of weeks. And please don't call me. I'll call you."

I hung up and turned off the phone, my heart pounding. I wiped the tears from my face and took a deep, cleansing breath. Richard could tremble and shake and bite his nails to the bone, but there was no way I'd be calling him until after my weekend with Zach.

My neck ached, I suddenly realized. Apparently, euphoria was only just keeping my tension at bay. I decided to drop my idea of picking up Thai food and just go home and have a hot soak. As I collected my belongings, a lavender flyer caught my eye. It was an advertisement for the women's yoga class down in the Kent Room, starting in half an hour.

Now there was an idea. In the whirlwind of wedding plans and the current crisis, I'd completely forgotten about Stephanie's yoga sessions. I could get some stretching in, then go home, climb in the bath, and call Zach for some bedtime talk. First, I'd need to change, which wasn't a problem. I slipped into my office's adjoining room and found some light blue leggings and a pale pink tank top.

I frowned at the sight of some of Lilah's work clothes on the floor. She must have been using my rug again for one of her shameless rendezvous. On closer inspection, I noticed my yellow sundress and a pair of sandals were missing. I'd have to get on her case about returning my stuff. Then I remembered what object of hers I'd been hoarding, and I blushed.

# Chapter 12
# Apres Yoga Rendezvous

**ANNEMARIE**

The Kent Room was all mirrors and gleaming wood floors. The hotel sponsored many exercise classes there from Zumba to strength training to Pilates. I'd done them all and found the Pilates to be most effective, but yoga was my favorite. Relaxing didn't come easy to me, so when I found something that worked, I was grateful.

Stephanie brightened when she saw me. "Annemarie." She reached out her arms for a hug. "It's so good to see you. How are things going?"

"Great," I said, smiling my biggest smile. I would have given that answer no matter what, but at least it wasn't a complete lie.

There were a few other women in the room, but it wasn't a big crowd, and I was glad. Individual attention from Stephanie was always welcome. I grabbed a purple yoga mat, a blanket, a strap, and a block.

The door swished open. It was Jenn. She still had her make-up on, and once again, I was amazed at how splendidly she got away with orange lips. She grinned when she saw me, waving and winking. "We meet again."

I found myself waiting to see where Jenn was going to claim her space. She picked the back of the room, and I unrolled my mat next to hers. She watched me as I did so, making me feel strangely self-conscious.

Stephanie started with meditative deep breathing in lotus position. I could feel the strain in my body melt away, my muscles grateful as we moved through dog, cobra, and tree. There was nothing like a good stretch. The feeling of letting go and opening up at the same time was something I didn't often experience. I had the other night with Richard, I realized, but I put it out of mind and instead thought about how I was about to really let go with Zach. The thought thrilled me, making me feel warm and sexy and ready.

"Excellent work," said Stephanie. "Now find a buddy." I glanced beside me at Jenn. She was giving me a questioning look that might have involved more than yoga poses.

I nodded, accepting her offer. I had wanted to give her a complete once over but felt too distracted before. Now I was totally present, and I took a good look at her. She wore pale yellow cotton pants that flared gently at the end, revealing tiny, feminine feet painted with coral polish that matched her lips. The waistband was rolled down, turning the pants into hip huggers. Her white tank was cut into a midriff, exposing her belly, which was surprisingly lush, given her slight frame. A thin, gold ring pierced her navel. I stole a look at her tiny, round breasts, the nipples apparent through thin cotton. The nape of her fine long neck glistened with just a touch of perspiration.

I forced my attention back to Stephanie, who was telling us how to spot each other for inverted poses, which were definitely not my favorite thing. Being upside down was a bit frightening for me, but going against the class was out of the question. "Wanna go first?" Jenn asked, the teasing gleam still in her eyes.

I nodded, thinking that getting it over with was the right idea. I kneeled, clasping my hands together to make a cradle for my head, then signaled to Jenn that I was ready. I felt her hands, small but strong, grab my legs firmly as I lifted them up. She held onto my thighs as I settled into the pose, her thumbs gently kneading the back of my legs. The sensation trickled along my body, landing, astonishingly, between my legs. I abruptly let myself down, imagining that I'd been thinking way too much about sex.

Jenn was smiling at me—she always was, it seemed—and I realized I liked her. This was about as likely as Titania falling for Bottom the Ass without any magical help. Was Zach my Oberon? Had he somehow enchanted me? Whatever the explanation, I was under the spell.

If Jenn's shirt hadn't been so tight, it would have totally exposed her breasts when she went upside down. As it was, I simply got to enjoy looking at their undersides while she luxuriated in headstand position. She was so good at it that I barely had to hold her at all. I just let my hands grasp her slender ankles lightly until she was done.

At the end of class she said, "Are you busy now?"

I thought about my hot soak and phone call to Zach. Both of them could wait. "No," I said.

"Wanna come over for a smoothie?"

Smoothie indeed. Turned out she was serious, because the first thing she did when we stepped into her apartment was open her fridge and unload a quart of vanilla yogurt, a package of strawberries, and a frozen banana. She packed the ingredients in the blender, throwing in a dollop of honey and some chia seeds, and let it whizz, then poured the concoction into two beer mugs and put them on the kitchen table.

I sipped the sweet, cold drink and watched Jenn take a big swig as though she were drinking an ice cold beer instead of a fruity health beverage. A mustache of pale pink stuff lingered on her upper lip, making her look like one of those sexy milk advertisements. "You have smoothie on you," I said.

"Darn," she said, giggling. "I'm all out of napkins."

"Just lick it off," I said.

"How?" she asked.

"Like this." I ran my tongue along my lip and the skin above it.

"I can't quite get what you're doing," she whispered. "Come a little closer and show me."

I couldn't believe I was playing this game, and I couldn't believe how much fun it was. I stood up and walked to Jenn's chair, kneeling beside her and putting my face close to hers. "Like this," I said, licking again.

"Do that to me," she said, her voice falling deeper into her chest.

I leaned forward, completely enticed by her scent, a mix of sweat, lavender, and strawberries. The smoothie was already warm by the time I lapped it off, but not nearly as warm as the inside of Jenn's mouth when she kissed me, slow, long, and sweet.

What the hell was happening to me? Jenn's lips were small but full, her kisses wet and probing and deliberate.

"Come on," she said, taking me by the hand and leading me into her bedroom. It was huge, and furnished like a jungle, with animal print curtains and sheets and masses of plush pillows. We lay on the giant mattress, embracing and making out for a long time. Jenn kissed my eyelids, nipped my earlobes, and licked the hollow of my neck. This was even more relaxing than yoga. I felt like I was floating on some kind of sensual cloud.

Then she took my hand and slipped it inside her shirt, placing it on one of her breasts. I rubbed the soft flesh, taking the erect nipple between finger and thumb, twisting and jiggling until she moaned quietly. I was amazed at how utterly natural it was. Jenn's breasts weren't like foreign objects I'd never encountered. Hadn't I done this to myself a million times over? Hadn't I played with my own nipples, reveling in the sensations and in the freedom from having a man there to please? I felt totally confident with Jenn. Making love to a woman felt like second nature.

The relaxed, floating feeling was giving way to something more hungry and urgent. I grabbed Jenn's shirt to pull it off. She obliged, lifting her arms. As I tossed the shirt away, she kept her arms in the air, making her tits completely and deliciously vulnerable. I accepted the offering greedily, lifting them in my hands and loving them with my mouth and tongue as Jenn stroked my hair, then reached down my back to pull up my shirt. When she saw my breasts, her eyes lit up. She immediately attacked them with her hands and mouth, all the while delivering a running monologue about how amazing they were.

In no time we were completely naked. Jenn's barely there bush was styled into a cute triangle. It couldn't hide the swollen nub of her clitoris, peeking out of her slit like a mischievous kid looking for fun and adventure. I tickled it, and she sat back against the head of the bed, opening her legs for more. I explored her sex with my hand, and Jenn moved her hips against me, encouraging me. I put two fingers inside her, and as I moved them in and out, I watched her body undulate.

Jenn pulled one of my arms toward her. "Kneel over me," she said, leaning over to open her night table drawer and take out a square of latex. "So I can lick you."

I placed my knees around her head and felt her warm breath between my legs. I was anticipating the feel of her tongue, but she surprised me by inserting a finger, hard and fast. The act was aggressive, primal, and totally hot. I let out a squeal of delight and Jenn laughed, pulling me closer to urge my head toward her sex. "Lick me," she said, handing me the square of latex in her hand and reaching into the drawer to grab another. I felt the dental dam press against my sex, then Jenn's mouth engulfed me. Oh, she knew what she was doing. She worked me with her finger and tongue, alternating them in a perfect rhythm. Every time her finger went inside me, her tongue flipped back to my clitoris, giving it a gentle suck.

I knew I was supposed to be returning the favor, but what I was receiving was too amazing, and besides, I didn't know what the hell to do with the piece of rubber she'd just handed me. So I just knelt there on the bed, over Jenn's face, moving my hips and moaning like an animal, coming hard in her mouth. "That's it," she mumbled, licking furiously.

I collapsed, resting my head on Jenn's mound, breathing hard. She didn't let up, though. Her fingers continued to probe inside me, slow and gentle, as though looking for something. When I started moaning again, she asked, "Is that the right place, hon?" I didn't know what she was talking about, really, and didn't answer. "Does that feel good?" she demanded.

This time I responded in the affirmative. It felt incredible. She continued to stroke me, finding erogenous zones I didn't know existed. Meanwhile, her enticing scent drifted toward me. The message was clear. I had to give back. I placed the latex awkwardly on her mound and began to kiss her. It was unfamiliar territory, but I welcomed it with my best effort. I wasn't nearly as skilled as Jenn, but I dabbed at her clitoris with my tongue, and sucked it gently and lovingly as my fingers moved inside her. It seemed to do the trick as it wasn't long before she was totally worked up, yelling "Oh, yes, baby," and throbbing with satisfaction.

No problems with sexual multi-tasking for Jenn—she'd been stroking me the whole time. Now she started tickling my anus, trying to get inside it with a gloved finger. I wasn't tied to the bed like I'd been the other night with Richard, but I still was in no position to stop her. Nor did I want to. Once she was inside both holes, I began to feel deep sensations of pleasure. I closed my eyes and rocked against Jenn's hands, opening my knees as wide as I could to give her total access. My conscious mind was way in the background, but it was telling me that I was feeling something familiar yet different—a sensation of needing to pee, but not quite the same as the usual signal. Jenn was talking to me the whole time, her words squelching any concerns my brain might have been alerting me to. "Don't hold onto it, baby. Let it run."

Suddenly I felt something like an orgasm, except so much more than that. Warm liquid flowed out of me, my whole body alive with pleasure and pulsation.

I opened my eyes, spent and exhilarated, and practically jumped out of my skin. There was a man standing at the foot of the bed. I certainly hadn't heard him come in, but he'd been watching the whole thing. Jenn was laughing underneath me, and he was smiling broadly. I got up off my hands and knees, grabbed a pillow, and hugged it to me. The man, who was wearing cargo pants and a tight black tank top, began to applaud quietly. "Very nice work, baby."

Jenn jumped up. As she planted a kiss on the man, I began to sense that something was amiss. When Jenn finished kissing him, she turned to come back to me on the bed. The man slapped her ass cheeks as she did, and she laughed again, heartily. She wrapped her arms around my trembling body and said, "Annemarie, this is Iona."

Iona nodded at me and held out her hand, looking into me with dark, intense eyes. "How do you do?"

I stared blankly, thinking Iona was like no man I'd ever met, then Jenn nudged me and said, "Come on, Annemarie. Shake her hand."

*Her* hand? Yes, most definitely her hand, I thought as I shook it and made some kind of pleasant, civilized response. Jenn pulled back the silky leopard sheets and said to me, "Wanna stay over?"

Before I had a chance to answer, Iona sat on the bed next to me and started stroking my hair. "Sure she does," she said. "Don't you, honey?"

I remembered Zach. I wanted to call him, but leaving didn't seem like an option. Besides, Iona didn't seem like she'd be happy with no for an answer, and for some strange reason, I found that I wanted to please her. "Yes," I said. "Of course."

I thought it was the right answer.

# Chapter 13
# Lilah's Wild Ride

**LILAH**

I'd never fucked blind before. As soon as Sue wrapped that black cloth around my eyes, I couldn't see a damn thing. Baby's little swing was on a pulley, and Prado had me jacked up so I was like a big old branch swaying in the breeze.

It put me in mind of Gina, my best friend when I was a teenager, who played Peter Pan in the high school musical. She was the first androgynous person I'd known, and my first pussy. Hiked up like that, I had a vision of Gina dangling in the air, singing *I Gotta Crow*.

Something large and slick entered me. I guessed it was the giant two-headed dildo I'd caught a glimpse of before the lights went out. "Mmmmm." That was Sue, and I couldn't tell whether she was humming as in *whistle while you work*, or moaning as in *wow, that's nice*. Prado started vocalizing, and he was definitely doing the latter. From the sounds he was making, I surmised he was partaking in more than just watching Sue go at me with her big toy.

I imagined what Prado might be up to, and that turned out to be pretty fun. As the dildo continued to fuck me at a gentle and remarkably steady pace, I pictured Prado stroking his gorgeous cock. I loved to see a guy play with himself, even if only in my mind. A small gurgle of pleasure escaped from my lips, but I was immediately silenced by a nasty slap on the ass. "No noise," said Sue firmly, then in a quiet croon, "Not until Mommy says so."

The dildo never stopped its smooth motions, nor did its timing waver. Mommy's like a goddamn machine, I thought, as my thighs were abruptly dropped and someone—Prado, probably, judging by the size of the hands and the fact that the damn dildo was still going—yanked my wrists behind me and tied them together with a piece of scratchy rope.

"Look at these beautiful titties," said Sue. Prado laughed in response. "Baby's such a big girl." Sue was in croon mode again. Big, fleshy fingers started pinching my nipples in the most delicious way. Had to be Prado, because the dildo was still fucking me, plus there was no trace of sharpness from Sue's daggers.

Truth to tell, I was a little scared, but overall, things were enjoyable. "Move," ordered Sue, and I didn't know who she was talking to until the hands—Prado's, most definitely—stopped playing with my tits and lowered me slightly. I felt the hint of a breeze and the sense of a warm body approaching, a body that was going to have its way with me. Sue (I was sure it was Sue) stepped closer.

The dildo stopped its continual, constant motion and moved as though it were being adjusted. Sue stepped close enough that I could feel the tips of her nipples brush against me. I realized she must be inserting the other end of the dildo into herself. In seconds I knew I was right. Her hands wrapped around my bare shoulders for leverage. Long fingernails tickled me as she came nearer and nearer, groaning like a sexy beast in heat. The front of her body was pressed against mine now, her floral scent like sweet nectar.

I imagined the dildo entering her deeply, as deeply as it was entering me, deeper and deeper the closer she came, a gigantic, massive cock joining us. Her bushy mound met mine, and I was shocked by its wiry feel. No longer controlled, she was gyrating and bouncing hard, smushing into me with abandon. Prado's big hands grabbed my ass and squeezed hard. He held me in place while Sue went wild, and encouraged her the whole time like a cheerleader.

There I was, dangling in the air and being fucked silly in the dark, sandwiched between the bodies of a famous rock star and his weird girlfriend. I might have laughed out loud if I thought good ol' Mommy would allow it, but really, I wanted to behave.

Sue's body quivered in orgasm and fell away from me, taking the big dildo with her. Now that I could feel my pussy open and exposed again, I felt the wave that had been building up during the fuck. It hadn't yet crested, and I hung there desperately wanting more, despite that raw pussy feeling that sometimes came after a good hammering. Mommy's cock, after all, had been huge.

So was Prado's, I remembered as Sue spoke to it in her little purr. "Look at Daddy's giant dick," she whispered. "You need some pussy, honey, don't you?" Someone worked the pulley so my feet were on the floor, then got me out of the swing. Turned out I'd been barely off the ground at all. Once I was standing, Sue's authoritative voice said, "Get on your knees." I obeyed, laying my face sideways on the carpet because my hands were still tied behind me. Almost instantly I was penetrated again. This cock was attached to its owner, who was most certainly Prado. He rammed me fast and hungrily, his big sack of balls knocking against the inside of my thighs.

It was a hard fuck, but I was enjoying it, so I was disappointed when Sue ordered it to stop. Awkward adjustments ensued. My blindfold was removed. My wrists, chafed and red, were freed. Things seemed unnaturally and harshly bright when I opened my eyes to my naked compatriots, who still looked damp and swollen with desire. Sue had donned a harness which supported a new dildo, this one sleek and long and red. It had a little wire attached to it, which led to a control panel Sue held in her hot little hand.

She pressed one button, then another, and I watched as the dildo vibrated, then rotated in tiny circles, then jerked in abrupt, short movements. Prado had taken a seat on the bed, and was rubbing his hard, purple dick with long, slow strokes. God, that was a beautiful sight. When Sue said, "Go suck Daddy," I was glad to do it. I leaned over Prado and breathed in the smell of stiff, moist, condomless cock. I wanted to say something about that, but before I could, Sue was pushing my head down, telling me to get started. I licked along Prado's shaft and around his head, holding him in one hand, gently opening his thighs with the other so I could give his balls a good tongue bath. He leaned back onto his elbows, sighing in contentment, while behind me, Sue positioned my ass as high in the air as it would go.

My mouth closed around Prado and I took the length of him in, sucking greedily. Sue's slick red dildo slipped inside my pussy, where it danced with all kinds of frequencies and undulations. I came almost immediately and might have taken a break from Prado, except he placed his hands squarely on my head and made it clear that I was to continue.

Sue had other ideas. "Sit on Daddy's lap," she said, backing away from my pussy. I could feel Prado's disappointment as I stood up, but there was no way he was going to defy Sue. "Face Daddy," said Sue. "I want to see your sweet little ass when you sit on him." I knelt over Prado on the bed, rubbing my wet slit against his cock because I didn't know whether Sue's command meant I should just sit on his cock or whether I should fuck him, and I really did want to be a good girl. Then she said, "Fuck Daddy," and I impaled myself on Prado.

He sucked at my nipples, driving me wild as I thumped on top of him. Sue slapped my ass and squeezed my cheeks, poking at my butthole with her cock. "Stop," she ordered, keeping me still long enough to slide her slim prick into my ass. To call it a wild ride would be an understatement. I'd never seen such a multi-faceted sex toy before, much less had one in my anus at the same time my pussy was filled with meaty cock.

I came again and was pretty much oblivious to anything but my tits and pussy and ass. Then Prado said, "Baby," and I knew he wasn't talking to me. "Baby, I wanna come." It was a desperate plea. Sue pulled her magic rod out of me and ordered me off Prado.

Things happened quickly after that. I'm not sure how, but in an instant, I was ushered out of our private sex den and back into the community orgy, which had waned but was still alive. Several people were sprawled on sofas and sheepskin rugs, sleeping. The man who'd been at the computer was getting sucked off by a young roadie. A Goth girl sat naked on a couch, her legs splayed wide, revealing a shaven, pierced pussy. The Eats drummer started fucking her, ramming her in rhythm to the music which was playing. It was Nirvana, but, I realized suddenly, I didn't feel at all heavenly.

The Goth girl was still, her tiny, black-tipped fingers absently playing with her nipple rings as she got thoroughly laid. She looked bored, or maybe I was just imagining it. The lead guitarist saw me and tried to lead me into the corner for some action, but I didn't want any more. In the span of one week, I'd had the wildest, most satisfying escapades of my long and gratifying sexual career. Apparently, that was enough for the moment.

I politely declined, and the guitarist went elsewhere. I put on my skort and tank top and looked at the clock. In this orgiastic cocoon, every shade was tightly drawn, so I hadn't even been able to tell that during my initiatory travels into spread-eagled flying, the sun had risen.

I made my way out of the Eats suite and down to the lobby, carefully sneaking out into the already sticky air. It was going to be a hot one. My body felt spent and strangely empty.

I ignored that and headed for home, doing my best to think of nothing but flour, sugar, butter and chocolate, and melting them into sweet, delicious creations, the rush of heat as the oven door opened, and standing by the streams of air from the whirring, bleating kitchen fans with Chad.

Despite its humidity, the fresh air cleared my head. I felt like I'd been living in a dream world for the past twenty-four hours, and in a way, I had. It was surreal and unwound me in ways I couldn't have predicted. From the day I'd accepted my insatiable bisexuality, I'd always managed to keep my feet on the ground. In that hotel suite with Prado and Sue, they had somehow, both literally and figuratively, gotten away from me. I had just sucked and fucked my favorite rock star, which should have left me feeling amazing, but instead, I felt overwhelmed. I'd even allowed it to happen without a condom, no-no number one in the polyamory playbook. As vulnerable as I felt, I might as well have been still swaying helplessly in Mama Sue's swing.

I was halfway home when I remembered Annemarie and the shit that was going down with her. I didn't want to see her at the moment. I turned into the café a block from our apartment. I could use an herbal iced tea, and I may as well check my phone, something I didn't do nearly often enough, as Annemarie was wont to remind me.

The café was a quaint little establishment. I felt sure the only reason it survived was because Penny, the owner, was so cool. She made sure everyone felt welcome. The place had an old-fashioned vibe that brought people back and made them regulars. Penny also made lattes that rivaled Starbucks and scones that even I could appreciate. I'd often thought of trying to land her a job in my kitchen, but I think I was afraid she might compete for mine. Besides, she was perfectly happy running her own business.

I walked in and found Penny to be bright and cheery despite the heatwave which turned most people into grumps. "Hey, Lilah." She greeted me with a smile and a hug. I ordered an iced tea and found a table, then looked at my phone. Only one text, from Jenn, apologizing for losing me and saying she'd see me at work. A flash of anger welled up inside me as I remembered her and Richard ditching me.

Just for kicks, I logged into my gmail account, which I rarely checked anymore. 374 unread messages. Most were spam, and the others were so outdated they were no longer relevant. When I got to the more recent messages, I saw one from an address I didn't recognize.

*Woodworker777* was about to be deleted into internet oblivion when my eye caught the subject line: *Message from Chad.* My skin got warm in a way that had nothing to do with the weather. I opened the message and read:

> *Hey Lilah,*
>
> *What happened the other night? Can we talk? Want to go hear some music on Friday? A friend of mine is doing a concert. See you in the kitchen*
>
> *— Chad*

I found myself ambivalent at the prospect. Of course I wanted to go, but after what happened with Chad last time, I was nervous. The truth was, I was used to being in charge on dates. It wasn't that I'd never been topped — although Iona was a first in many ways, that wasn't one of them. But it had been a long time since I'd dated anyone who didn't follow my confident lead, and Chad definitely had not. Not only that, he seemed to have some issue with the way I left him behind on the dance floor.

Hopefully I hadn't blown it. The man was a puzzle. How could I lead when I didn't know what the heck he wanted? Clearly it wasn't sex, or at least not just sex. Had I ever gone out with anyone who didn't make fucking a priority? Heck, had I ever made anything but fucking a priority? There was Patrick, whom I'd dated for months in culinary school. He was my friend first, before we became lovers. Ironically, it was during my relationship with him that I defined myself as a bi, poly woman interested in multiple partners. He got a job at a swanky restaurant on the West coast, and we lost touch shortly after graduating.

I missed him, I realized with a sudden shock. I hadn't had such significant talks with anyone since then. Annemarie came the closest, but a lot of the time we talked about guys, and in those conversations I was usually lording my sexual superiority over her, if only in my mind. We'd had some discussions about serious issues, like climate change, which was one of those things she worried about and I tried not to think about, and sexism at work. I loved impassioned, intelligent conversations as much as the next gal, but for me, they were intellectual exercises, never personal, and while I had no trouble talking about things that other people considered private and intimate (like sex), I rarely opened up about my feelings to anyone.

One of the reasons for that may have been the fact that until that moment in the café, I hadn't been consciously aware of something fundamental about my own life. I was lonely. How could that be possible? I'd worked hard to create the life I wanted, or thought I wanted, one full of lovers, excitement, the thrill of the chase, and the satisfaction of conquest after conquest. So what was wrong now? I thought of Richard, who, despite displaying some real jerk behavior of late, was also being brave and trying to grow. Was his soul searching setting me off somehow? No, I decided. I was perfectly happy and satisfied with my life. Too much sex was the problem. Too much of a good thing could happen to anyone, and it had happened to me. A short stint (very short) of celibacy, with lots of meditation and yoga and a few good books, would renew me.

It may have been a crazy plan, but I decided to try it. The question remained—should I go out with Chad, especially under those conditions? Part of me wanted to deny him, to play hard to get and make him suffer for refusing me the first time. After all, if he'd only done what he was supposed to, I'd have been basking in the glow and hotness of a new lover instead of falling into adventures that turned out to be too much, even for me. As soon as I had the idea, though, I nixed it. Chad wasn't a game player. The realization came to me with a huge wave of relief. It also made another thing clear. I could go out with Chad without fucking him.

I composed a reply to his message:

*Hey,*

*Yeah, sorry about the other night. I'd love to get together, Friday sounds good. See you in a bit — we're making profiteroles, my favorite*

*— Lilah*

I sat back in my chair and took a deep breath, thinking of cream puffs laced with chocolate and how much I was looking forward to making them with Chad.

# Chapter 14
# Dinner with Joanne

## ANNEMARIE

Staying overnight with Jenn and Iona made me feel like a kid discovering cotton candy for the first time, and hanging out all day at the cotton candy machine, and eating and eating and loving every minute of it, until the inevitable tummy ache.

It wasn't about regrets, really, but when the morning light hit my eyes and I saw Jenn's head lying on my stomach, fast asleep, and Iona's impressive and intimidating frame spread out next to mine, snoring, I freaked out.

I could have let the feeling run away with me, which would have resulted in *me* running away, but I didn't get as far as I had by doing things that way. I had always embraced mastery, and I knew from experience that the most important moments to hang in there were the most tumultuous ones. So I let myself feel the panic, I let it seep through me in its torturous way, and just closed my eyes and breathed while my heart pounded and a knot welled up in my stomach like a cold, hard walnut.

After a few minutes, I recognized the feeling. It was the same one I'd had my first day on the job as Guest Relations Director when the end-of-afternoon tally showed I'd overspent the budget by a few hundred dollars. It was the one I'd had a few hours after accepting Richard's marriage proposal in the middle of dinner at Chef Wong's when I'd ordered a second plate of Lo Mein to celebrate and ate the whole damn thing.

I tended to be enthusiastic. I tended to overshoot. It didn't mean anything was actually wrong. Take my job and Richard, my self-talk pointed out. Both of those had turned out great—well, notwithstanding the current situation with Richard, the outcome of which remained to be seen.

The thing with Jenn and Iona had been fun. That I couldn't deny as I lay underneath Jenn and pondered it. Lilah would be delighted, or shocked, or both. She had no idea about my (admittedly minimal) dalliances with girls in college, and she'd been teasing me about Jenn's crush on me for a long time. If I were being perfectly honest with myself (I certainly wasn't going to be honest about it with anyone else), I had indulged in a few fantasies about her.

Now whatever fantasies I'd entertained had turned into a sweaty, fleshy, sexy reality, and gone beyond anything I could have dreamed up. It was a little intense, this new found pleasure, coming on the heels of Richard's crisis and my budding affection for Zach. I'd stay and see how things felt when Jenn and Iona awoke. Besides, leaving without a word while the people you just had sex with slept was simply bad form, and having just experienced it, I wasn't eager to inflict such thoughtlessness on anyone else.

My phone rang. I heard it faintly jangle, muffled from being buried inside my yoga bag. As gently as I could, I lifted Jenn's head and moved it off my body, to the side of the bed where Iona wasn't. Both of them stirred slightly but didn't wake, and I sat up and scooted myself to the end of the bed, then scrambled to find my bag and frantically dug through it for my phone, answering without even looking to see who was calling.

"Hello," I whispered, running into the kitchen to try and keep from being heard.

"Good morning."

It was Zach. The sound of his voice made my body feel like a lantern lighting up from the inside. "Hi."

I could hear the smile in his voice when he said, "You sound very awake."

"You didn't wake me up, if that's what you mean," I said.

"I confess," he answered. "I'd hoped to catch you still in bed."

"Why?" I whispered, not revealing the fact that he'd done exactly that.

"Why?" he repeated, his voice infused with sexiness, "So I could tell you all the things I want to do with you."

"That wouldn't be fair," I said, "hearing that all by my lonesome."

"Mmm," he said. "I imagine you'd have to do something about it. At least that's what I was hoping."

"Because you want to listen?" I asked, thinking that he was going ahead with his plan regardless, and judging by the warm feeling between my legs, it was working pretty darn well.

"But of course," he whispered. At that point I couldn't help myself from moaning just a little. My fingers were already moving to remedy the desire Zach had stirred up, as I had every intention of giving him what he wanted, when two strong hands wrapped around my waist from behind and Iona's voice growled a good morning into my ear.

That saying about the best laid plans was becoming the story of my life.

"Annemarie?" Zach's voice rose a couple of pitches, the hot, husky whisper gone.

"I'm here," I said.

Iona said, "Who is that getting you out of bed so early?" I barely had time to cover the phone with my hand to keep Zach from hearing what she said.

I wiggled out of Iona's clutches and took the phone into the bathroom, making apologetic gestures with my hands while closing the door behind me. "Zach?" I said.

"I'm here," he said, sounding brisk and professional. "I'm sorry, you're busy."

"I'm not," I said. "Really, I'm not. I'm just at a friend's house. We're about to have breakfast."

"I'll let you go, then," said Zach.

After a short, awkward silence, I said, "Why did you call?" It was a dumb thing to say, because it did nothing to underline the fact that I was very glad he'd called.

"As it turns out," he said. "Joanne and I are coming into town a day early."

"A day early?" I did the mental calculations. "That means—tomorrow."

"That's right," he laughed. "Tomorrow. I was hoping you could have dinner with us."

"Us?"

"Yes. Me, and Joanne."

"You want me to meet your wife? Already?"

"I'd love you to meet her," he said. "And she wants to meet you."

Of course he'd tell his wife about me, that's what polyamorous people did, but I didn't expect to actually meet her, at least not before Zach and I made love. "Is this part of the deal?" I asked.

"What deal?"

"I mean, part of the package, of, you know, being with you."

"I told you that Joanne and I always meet each other's partners."

"Right," I said. "I wasn't sure when that happened."

Zach laughed. "With us, it happens before physical intimacy. That's part of *our* deal." He paused, and his voice got husky again. "And I'm looking to mitigate any delays on that score."

My head was spinning, trying to figure out how I felt about this. Meeting Zach's wife didn't sound sexy or romantic, just awkward and terrifying. On the other hand, it sounded like I wasn't going forward with Zach until that little detail got out of the way. "What time?" I asked.

"It'll have to be early," said Zach. "Five? At Rudolph's?"

A banging sounded on the door. "I need to pee, Annemarie." It was Jenn.

"I'm sorry," I said, letting her in. To Zach I said, "I'll see you there."

When I got to Rudolph's the next day, Joanne and Zach had already arrived and were sitting at a corner table. Zach was facing me, and when I saw him, my heart skipped a beat. He was smiling, deep in conversation with his wife, his gorgeous, strong hands gesturing meaningfully, helping to convey his points.

As I stood there watching him, wondering what he might be talking about (and perhaps avoiding the inevitable for just a minute or two), he saw me. Our eyes locked, and his face changed. What did I see there? Excitement, warmth, caring, and for a fleeting second, heat. The only person who looked at me that way was Richard, but with time passing, and familiarity, and our busy lives, it happened less and less. Or did I just not notice?

I put Richard out of my mind and smiled at Zach. The woman with him—his wife, I reminded myself—turned around. She didn't look the way I thought she would. What had I expected, anyway? Someone who looked a little more like me, perhaps, and she definitely did not fit that bill. She was considerably older than I was, even older than Zach if my judgment was correct. Her brown eyes glowed and shimmered almost as much as the tiny opal embedded in the side of her petite, pierced nose. The life force she exuded was more extroverted than Zach's but just as strong. *Geez*, I thought. *Talk about a power couple.* They really did look like they belonged together.

Gazing upon their epic coupledom gave me a sudden longing for Richard, and with it, a good dose of terror at what I'd just walked into, but Zach and Joanne were both smiling and waving at me, and short of running away, I couldn't avoid the confrontation any longer. I took a deep breath and headed for the corner, then found myself in another awkward situation. Zach and Joanne were at a table for four, across from each other. Did I sit next to him, or next to her? As I was pondering, Zach stood and graciously pulled out the chair next to his.

I took it, relieved. Sitting beside him was my preference. Once I was settled, he slipped his hand under the table and took mine, squeezing. It was a sweet gesture, reassuring rather than sexual. I squeezed back, surprised at how much more comfortable holding Zach's hand made me feel. He said, "Annemarie, this is Joanne, my wife."

Joanne smiled and reached across the table. I shook her outstretched hand with my free one. It was a good handshake, and oddly, that moment of being physically connected to both of them made me feel even more relaxed. "Hi," Joanne said. "It's so wonderful to meet you." She was smiling, and though I couldn't quite believe it, my read on her said she was absolutely sincere.

"You, too," I said shyly. What else would I, or could I, say?

The waiter arrived and asked whether I wanted a drink. I ordered white wine. Zach was drinking red, and Joanne had a sparkling water with lime. "Zach tells me you work at The Sentinel," she said.

"I do."

"That's a great hotel," said Joanne. "I've stayed there many times." She was still smiling—she smiled a lot. When she did, tiny wrinkles sprouted around her eyes. You had to look to see them, as well as the gray flecks peppering her short, jet black hair.

"Really?" I answered. If she'd stayed at The Sentinel and I hadn't met her, it meant that she wasn't demanding. With her allergies, that seemed unlikely.

"Yes," she said, "but not for a few years. My company used to have a second headquarters here, but we moved it to Virginia a while back."

"We?" I said.

"Joanne owns her own company," said Zach.

"Like you," I said, turning to him.

"Sort of," he answered, sipping his wine. "Except hers makes way more money."

Inwardly, I rolled my eyes. My salary was perfectly acceptable as far as I was concerned, but they undoubtedly both earned a lot more than I did. "Are you complaining?"

"Absolutely not," said Zach. "I love the music business, even if it is imploding."

I turned to Joanne and asked, "What's your business?"

"I own a restaurant chain. We specialize in patty melts."

"Really?" I said again. I couldn't seem to muster many other words in this conversation.

"Patty Pete's," said Zach. "Perhaps you've heard of it."

I practically choked on my white wine. "Really?" The word came out of my mouth, laden with astonishment, before I could stop it. Just like that, I was embarrassed, and turning red.

Fortunately, Joanne was a very laid-back, gracious person. "Yup," she said, laughing. "Family business. I inherited it."

"And she's done a damn good job running it, too," said Zach with obvious pride.

"Thank you, darling," Joanne replied, with obvious affection. All this while Zach kept a firm, attentive hold on my hand under the table. A week ago, if someone had said the word *polyamory* to me I would have scoffed in disdain, but Zach and Joanne clearly had a respectful, caring relationship. She turned her attention to me. "So you're going to the cottage," she said.

"Cottage?" I knew Zach wanted to go away for the weekend, but we hadn't cemented any plans yet.

"I meant to talk to you about it yesterday morning," said Zach. "But you were busy. We have a cottage in New Hampshire. It's one of my favorite places."

"Really?" I said, again failing to muster anything more appropriate, something like, *that sounds delightful.* Which it did. My family used to go to New Hampshire when I was a child, and I hadn't been in years.

"We could do something else," said Zach. "If you prefer."

"No," I said. Escaping the complexity of the city — and my life — for a couple of days sounded perfect. I'd already put in for some vacation time and given Carol detailed instructions about the weekend guests. I didn't have to be back at work until Tuesday.

"You'll love it," Joanne said. "It's a fabulous place."

Our food arrived — Cobb salad for me, steak for Zach, and rice and steamed veggies for Joanne. I poured oil and vinegar on my salad and tossed it while Zach started cutting his steak and Joanne pulled a package of gluten free soy sauce out of her purse. It struck me as funny, suddenly, that although she owned Patty Pete's, she couldn't eat there, but I supposed it wasn't much different than my aversion to staying at hotels.

The conversation slowed a bit once the eating started, but it improved content wise. We talked about the food and hotel industries, and one of my pet peeves, the rampant sexism inherent therein. Joanne had a lot of ideas about it, and she got invited to business schools to talk about them. She was pretty damn cool, and I liked her a lot.

When the waiter cleared our plates and asked whether we wanted dessert and coffee, I requested a menu. He went to get it, and Joanne said, "Well, this has been lovely. I need to go. I have to be at a conference in New York bright and early."

"Really?" Unbelievably, I'd said it again, and even more unbelievably, I felt disappointed that she was leaving. She stood up, then Zach did, and I did, too. Joanne hugged Zach first, a long, heartfelt hug, then their lips touched and she said, "See you in a few days, love."

She turned to me. "Annemarie, it's been such a pleasure."

"Thank you," I said. "It was nice meeting you." I would have uttered the polite cliché regardless, but never in a million years had I expected to mean it.

She hugged me warmly. "Have a wonderful weekend," she whispered, her eyes sparkling.

"You, too," I said.

"Oh, I will," she answered with a wicked smile worthy of Lilah. She may have been going to a conference, but I guessed that wasn't all she had planned.

The key lime pie was mediocre, nowhere near as good as Lilah's. Zach seemed to like it, or maybe he just liked that I was feeding him. "Joanne must enjoy her job," I said. "She seemed awfully excited about that conference."

Zach laughed. "She does enjoy her work," he said. "But she has a good friend in New York, too."

"Friend, eh? Is that what you'll be calling me?"

He dropped his playful tone and that look of heat came back into his eyes. "No, Annemarie. Most definitely not."

I felt myself get warm inside. It felt reckless and good. "So when are we leaving on this little trip?" I asked.

Zach looked at his watch. "It's only six," he said. "We could go now and be there by ten."

"Now?" I asked. At least I hadn't said *really* again.

Zach smiled, nodding his head and running his fingers through his tousled hair. God, he was good looking.

"I really like Joanne," I said.

"Mmm," he agreed. "She's pretty awesome."

"Can we stop at my place so I can pack?"

"Of course," he said. "We do have to discuss a few things, though." I bristled, wondering what this could mean. Zach pulled some papers out of a briefcase and handed them to me. "My only sexual partner for the last six months has been Joanne," he said. "She, of course, has had others, but we always practice safe sex. These are the results of my most recent test results." I stared at the papers. They were certainly comprehensive. I saw negative results for AIDS, gonorrhea, and a few other STDs. "I understand this might be uncomfortable," Zach continued. "But it's important."

I looked at him. "I'm supposed to tell you about my sex partners?" I asked, thinking of my recent romp with Jenn and Iona.

"Not if you don't want to," he said. "But I would like you to share test results. Of course, no matter what, we'll practice safe sex."

I nodded. This was wise, very wise, but I still felt terribly uncomfortable. I pulled up an e-mail on my phone. "Here," I said, showing him the results of the blood tests I'd gotten when Richard and I had first started dating. They were still buried in my inbox, even if they weren't terribly recent.

Zach nodded. "Thanks," he said. "Joanne and I make it a practice to get tested every six months. How do you feel about that?"

I felt numb about it. I hadn't gotten to the point of thinking practically about what a polyamorous lifestyle would mean. It looked so good on Zach and Joanne. Lilah and Jenn seemed to do it relatively painlessly, although I had to admit that based on my observations of Lilah, it created more drama than a person like me tended to want in her life. If I was going to go forward, however, Zach's proposition made sense, and the level of responsibility with which he and Joanne structured their relationship was reassuring. I nodded again. Zach squeezed my hand, and I slipped out of the rental car and into my apartment building.

# Chapter 15
# A Weekend at the Cottage

**ANNEMARIE**

While Zach waited, I ran inside to grab a few belongings. I'd given up the elevator as part of my fitness pledge, and as I climbed the three flights to the apartment, I considered the inventory of items I needed to pack. I didn't plan to bring much, just a few pairs of panties, my black lace nightie, some casual clothes for walks or hanging out, and my toothbrush, some toiletries, and make-up.

Unfortunately, Lilah was home. "Hey," she said when she saw me. "Where have you been?"

"Out," I said. I didn't have the time or inclination to come up with a story, and at the moment, I didn't feel like the truth was any of her business. She followed me into my bedroom and watched as I pulled my overnight bag out of my closet. "Going somewhere?"

I nodded. "I need to get away for a few days."

"Where are you going?"

"To stay with a friend."

Lilah was standing way too close to me, paying way too much attention to what I was packing. "Who?"

"Just a friend," I said. My last item was the nightie, but I didn't want Lilah to see that.

"Bullshit," said Lilah. "Annemarie, what the hell is going on?"

"Look, Lilah," I said, opening the drawer with my negligees and pulling out two, the black one and the cream one. She was acting way too entitled, and I didn't care anymore what she saw. Besides, I needed to get the hell out of there fast. Lilah's presence and its reminders of the rest of my life were giving me second thoughts. I slung my bag over my shoulder. "I'll tell you all about it when I get back."

Lilah followed me to the door most unhappily. "Are you going with Richard? Is that why you have those nightgowns? Just tell me." I scoffed, a little too angrily. Lilah stood at the door, blocking me. "So, not Richard? Who then? Who the fuck are you spending the weekend with and why won't you talk to me?"

"Get out of my way, Lilah," I said, a little too loudly. She was acting like I was doing something unbelievable and rash, and maybe I was, but it was something I wanted to do and was going to do, and I didn't want to be set on the path of thinking about consequences at the moment.

"Baby," said Lilah, and I cringed. She never called me that. "I'm sorry things are so messed up. Please just tell me where you're going so I won't worry."

I looked at her. "That's the only reason you want to know?"

She stiffened for a split second before saying, "I'm worried about you."

I felt my insides sink into helpless mush. "I'm worried about me, too," I said, and hugged her for a long time before gently pushing Lilah aside and slipping out the door. "I'll be back in a couple of days," I called as I left, bounding down the stairs two at a time.

"That was quick," said Zach when I got back to the car.

"Really?" I said. It didn't feel quick.

"Everything okay?" asked Zach.

I nodded and smiled reassuringly. Once we were cruising on the highway, I took out my phone—fourteen texts. Fortunately, only one was from Richard who'd figured out that frantic and desperate didn't look good on him.

*Thinking of you, missing you. Call me soon. XOXO*

He was sounding more like his usual self, and I smiled at the sweetness of the message and the tingly thrill it gave me, which coexisted right alongside the terror that I was doing something exceedingly foolish, destroying any chances of the wedding going off as planned, throwing my life away. I looked at Zach's quiet, serious profile. How could I still have such deep feelings for Richard and yet be so smitten with Zach? Then there was the pure unadulterated sex fun I'd had with Iona and Jenn the night before. *Lilah would so proud of me*, I thought with an inward smirk, but the fact was that while I was having fun, maybe too much fun, I was also terribly confused, and I didn't have a lot of experience with that kind of feeling.

I looked back at the texts. There was one from Jenn, saying what a good time she'd had and that she hoped she'd see me again soon. Most were from Carol who wasn't quite as self-sufficient as I wanted her to be. I took a bit of time to answer her questions, sent a quick text to Jenn thanking her for her hospitality, and texted Lilah not to worry, that I'd be back Sunday or Monday. Then I turned off the phone, resolving to leave it that way until I got home.

When we stepped through the front door of the cottage I took a deep, cleansing breath worthy of one of Stephanie's yoga cool downs. The place smelled slightly musty and very woody. Sand and grit crunched under my flip flops as I walked across the floorboards. It was dark, and I bumped into a bulky piece of furniture—a tattered old couch, I discovered as Zach flicked on the light.

Well, well. This was nothing like The Sentinel. In fact, it was very much like the small place my family rented when I was a little girl, and suddenly fond memories of the lake, the mountains, and getting tucked into bed at night overcame me.

The large lamps sitting on wooden side tables, the fireplace with the generous pile of wood stacked neatly beside it, and the magazines strewn on the maple coffee table were just so retro, so slow. I felt my anxiety recede a bit.

Zach came up behind me and wrapped an arm around my waist. "It's nothing fancy," he whispered in my ear.

His warm breath sent shivers through me. "It's perfect," I said.

Zach took my hand and said, "Let me show you around."

There wasn't much to see. In addition to the large living room, there was an eat-in kitchen with a linoleum floor and an old Formica table and chairs, a bathroom, and a small first-floor office which, I saw, was where the technology resided. "We try not to use this room much," said Zach, closing the door. I wondered who *we* meant—him and Joanne? Him and one of his other lovers?

At the top of a flight of stairs so steep and low-ceilinged that Zach had to duck were three bedrooms. Two were tiny and held nothing but twin trundle beds and small dressers, but the master bedroom was a decent size, big enough for a king size bed and the largest chifferobe I'd ever seen. The room had its own bathroom, which was the most modernized room in the cottage, with a pair of sinks and a gigantic triangular bathtub. My eyes lit up when I saw it. Oh, this was going to be fun.

Zach was behind me, and either he was a mind reader or my eyes lighting up were reflected in the shining white porcelain, because he said, "I like it, too."

I turned and raised an eyebrow at him. "Actually, I feel kind of dirty right now."

He faced me, wrapping his strong arms around my waist and moving his face close to mine. "Is that so?" he whispered, and I jumped when his hand unexpectedly grabbed a chunk of my behind and squeezed hard. "I feel dirty, too."

I playfully smacked his arm and said, "I wasn't talking about that kind of dirty."

"Oh, really," he crooned, running his full lips along my neck in the most teasing and tantalizing way. "I think you're just looking for an excuse to get into that tub with me."

"Busted," I whispered.

To my dismay, he let go of me and said, "We have all night, and I'd like to talk awhile first. Let's go downstairs." Talking was the last thing I wanted to do, but Zach wasn't making straight up escape from my problems an option.

Mystified and horny, I followed him.

I sat on the lumpy couch while Zach turned down the lamp light and lit a few candles. "I'll be right back," he said, disappearing into the kitchen. I listened to the sounds of a cabinet opening, glasses clinking, the creak of the refrigerator door, and the pop of a cork. He wasn't hurrying, that's for sure. I took another deep breath and reminded myself to stop trying to make things happen, to just relax and let them.

Zach returned with two glasses of chilled white wine, handed me one, then snuggled in close beside me. I took a sip. It was delicious, crisp and light. Zach smiled and I thought I'd melt into a puddle. "Your smile is a lethal weapon, you know that?" I teased him.

He laughed. "I could say the same of yours."

"Well," I said. "We'll just have to be careful not to do too much damage." Inwardly, I slapped myself. Just what was that unromantic statement about?

"Are you scared?" he asked quietly.

This was serious Zach, and the depth of sincerity was as powerful as sexy Zach. But did I want that? What did I want? It was unlike me not to know. "Yes," I answered, meaning it.

"That's okay," said Zach. "I am, too."

"You?" I asked, incredulous.

"Tell me about your fiancé," he said. "What's happening?"

I really hadn't come there to talk about Richard, but for some reason that made no logical sense, I felt comfortable doing it with Zach. "I don't know," I said, and the words were loaded with so many things, and suddenly all those things emerged from the very closed boxes I'd been keeping them in, into my heart, my mind, and into my eyes, where they expressed themselves in what felt like it was going to be an endless stream of tears.

Zach didn't say anything while I cried, just put down his glass of wine and wrapped his arms around me.

I don't know how long I sobbed, but when I finally lifted my head from his shoulder, there was a big damp splotch on his shirt. "I'm sorry," I said, rubbing the wet spot as though I could make it go away.

Zach laughed. "Always trying to take care of things," he said.

"It's my job," I answered by way of explanation.

"And you do it so well," said Zach. My hair, I realized, had also fallen prey to the multitude of tears. I felt it matted to my cheek as though pasted there. Before I had a chance to worry about how that looked, Zach's hand gently brushed it back behind my ear. "I want you to take care of yourself just as painstakingly," he said.

"Don't I?" The question, spoken out loud, was meant more for me than for Zach. He seemed to realize it, and stayed quiet. "I love Richard," I whispered. This was not the right thing to say to get Zachary Link in bed, but other things seemed more important at the moment.

"I know," said Zach. "What's going on?"

I shrugged. "He wants to talk to me. He sounds scared."

"Of losing you? I can understand that."

"But the whole thing is his fault. He's the one who said he needed space."

"But why," said Zachary. "The question is why."

"I have no idea." I could hear the bewilderment and exasperation in my own voice.

"Haven't you talked to him?"

I shook my head. "Not yet."

"Why?" I didn't answer, not sure of the reason myself. "Are you trying to punish him?"

That statement felt like a punch in the gut, one that was full of painful truth. Tears started welling up again. "Maybe," I said.

"That's my fear," he said softly. "That you're just here to get to him."

"Oh, no," I said immediately. "Not just that." Whoa. Did I say that out loud? Did I speak those words to Zachary Link? They were true, though, I realized. At least part of the reason I'd been in high sex mode was to spite Richard, and in some kind of weird, controlling way, keep myself from being devastated by him.

Zach's beautiful face fell. "Not just," he repeated, and turned away.

"I'm sorry," I said. "I didn't mean that." It was lame damage control. Where had my talents gone?

Zach still wasn't looking at me, but he squeezed my hand. "Don't do that, Annemarie."

"Do what?"

"Pretend. I know you're trying to protect me, but the only way we're going to protect each other is with honesty." He turned back to face me. "It makes sense that you'd have those feelings."

"Thank you," I said. "For understanding."

He smiled. "But I can't let myself be used. Or hurt, if I can help it." The idea that I could hurt Zachary Link was so unlikely. He seemed to read my thoughts. "Yes, Annemarie. I am vulnerable. With you."

My heart melted. I just wanted to hold him, kiss him, and make love to him. Instead, I started crying again. "This is very confusing. I love Richard, so how can I feel this way about you?"

Zach held me again and said, "Our hearts are capable of a lot of love,

Annemarie."

*He's right,* I thought as I buried my face against his warm, inviting body. *He's so completely right.*

We stayed in the living room for awhile longer, until when I didn't know. I didn't bother checking the clock. Time kind of stopped as we hung out.

It felt great, and natural, and so did the moment when we found ourselves looking into each other's eyes, both of us knowing that right here, right now, this is the time to kiss, and we did, each of us leaning toward the other, meeting halfway in the space between us, my lips finding his, so soft, so warm, then our tongues, so hot, so wet.

I hadn't enjoyed such an extended make-out session for a very long time, but there was no need to rush things. Time had ceased to exist, and we were getting to know each other, in more ways than one.

"Annemarie," Zach whispered. "You're so beautiful."

I only moaned in response. His breath in my ear, and his tongue licking my earlobe, precluded my saying anything coherent.

He pulled away and took off his shirt, and the sight of his bare, perfect chest and the tiny ripples in his abdomen sent warm rushes through my body. "Take off your dress," he said. "Now."

It reminded me of Richard ordering me around the last time we were together, and how surprisingly sexy I'd found it. This, too, was sexy. Sexy as hell. I obeyed and didn't stop there. As I slipped off my panties, Zach took off his jeans and his boxers, and I gasped at the sight of him naked, his strong legs, his generous erection. "Stand up," he said.

I stayed still and watched him examine every inch of my body, his appreciation apparent in his eyes. He reached out and lightly cradled one of my breasts in his hand. "So, so beautiful," he murmured. I closed my eyes as his other hand reached out and he caressed both my breasts, so expertly, so tenderly, gently pinching and kneading my nipples, sending me into a frenzy of desire.

I wanted to grab onto him, kiss him long and hard, but before I could make a move he'd scooped me into his arms and carried me up, up, up the steep staircase, into the bedroom.

The peach silk sheets felt deliciously smooth underneath me but nowhere near as delicious as the feel of Zach's skin on mine, covering every inch of me, his erection pressing on the mound of my sex like a big tease.

I opened my legs and reached down to take him in my hand. He moaned as I stroked him, so big, so solid, so good. I wanted him in my mouth first, then inside me. I gently pushed him onto his back, kissing his neck, his gorgeous chest, his exquisite stomach, licking the inside of his thighs, the dampness of his balls, the length of his sex.

"Oh, Annemarie," he whispered. "Annemarie." I lifted my head to look at him. He was watching me—he liked to watch, too. It thrilled me.

"You want to see me suck you?" I asked, shocking myself.

"Yes," he said, stroking the back of my head with urgency, exerting an almost imperceptible pressure downward, and handing me a condom from the night table next to the bed.

I rolled on the condom and took him in my mouth, running my tongue along his shaft. He relaxed as I worked him with my mouth. When I felt his readiness, I let go and held him in my hand as he spurted into the condom.

He reached down and grabbed me, squeezing me tight in his arms, then guiding me down on the bed just as I'd done to him, kissing my entire body, making me crazy with anticipation and desire. He slipped a finger inside me and I groaned. "You're so wet, Annemarie," he said, breathing on my sex, and I thought I could come from that alone. He took another condom from the night table, then opened the drawer and pulled out a tiny pair of scissors, which he used to cut the condom into a square. It took all of about thirty seconds, which was thirty seconds longer than I wanted to wait to feel his mouth on me. When it finally got there, I exploded immediately, and he held my hips as my whole body shook with release.

He put one finger back inside me, then another "I didn't get enough of a taste," he said, gently licking between my legs. "I want more." His nose nuzzled my clitoris, drawing from it an even deeper level of desire.

I grabbed onto his head and pushed his face into me as he took my clitoris into his mouth and sucked it.

Another wave built inside me, I felt almost delirious as it grew, then crested.

I exploded again, my release accompanied by wild, joyous screaming.

Later, we emerged from the bed and got into that glorious tub.

I stepped into the water first as Zach lit the candles situated around the edges. He liked candles, apparently. I didn't mind. They were romantic, and just enough light to see by. I still didn't know what time it was, but outside it was still dark. Remarkable, how long and luscious a night could be.

The water swayed gently as Zach got in the tub. I spied his rekindled erection before it disappeared under the surface, and smiled. I had my own version of one down there, too. "Annemarie," he whispered, taking me in his arms and kissing me. "Lovely Annemarie." Our bodies were radiating desire, but being submerged seemed to call for slowness. Slow kissing, slow rubbing up against each other, slow fondling.

"You feel so good," I said finally, not able to wait any longer. He knew what I was feeling, as he so often did, and stood up to slip on a condom. I pulled myself up and sat on the edge of the tub, opening my legs to receive him. He slipped inside me, and I cried out at as he filled me up. "Zach." I breathed hard in his ear, licking the edges gently.

I lifted my bottom and let the length of him, all but the tip, slide out, then ever so slowly I moved down again, feeling every sensation of every inch so exquisitely completely. Zach groaned, and his desire urged me on. I picked up the pace, and he kissed me, moving with me, until water splashed around us, dousing the candles.

"Come, Annemarie," Zach cried. "Come now."

I did, and we climaxed together, panting and holding each other, sinking down into the warm, still water.

# Chapter 16
# A First Date

LILAH

When I got to work, Chad was already there. "Still reading that book?" I asked as I unlocked the kitchen door.

"Yeah," he said, closing *Anna Karenina* and stuffing it in his backpack. "It's long."

"Why that book?" I asked, flicking on the kitchen light.

"I finally got around to seeing the movie on Netflix and decided it was time to re-read the book."

"The one with Keira Knightley?"

"Mmm, hmm," he said, smiling. "Did you see it?"

"No," I answered. I didn't get to the movies too often, but I had wanted to see that one. "Was it good?"

"The way they filmed it was cool," said Chad. "But my favorite part of the book isn't Anna, it's Levin."

I dug deep in my memory, way back to my world literature class at college. "Levin. The guy who lives in the country?"

"Yes," said Chad.

"Why do you like him so much?"

"Well, he's in love and searching for answers, just like Anna," Chad said, "but he doesn't lose himself."

"But he's a rich guy, and Anna is a woman forced to be dependent on men for everything. It's not a fair comparison."

"True," said Chad, smiling widely. He seemed to like this conversation.

"Hey, kids. How goes it?" Jenn walked in looking exhausted but sated, or maybe I was just projecting what I assumed she'd be feeling.

"I'm great," I said icily. "You look tired. Long night?"

She came up behind me and gave me one of her sweet hugs. "Lilah," she said, a bit too intimately. "I missed you last night."

Chad was watching us, looking, I thought, slightly uncomfortable. I pulled away and tried to change the subject. "The concert rocked, huh?"

"Amazing," said Jenn, smiling widely.

"Who did you see?" asked Chad.

"The Eats," said Jenn. "They were unbelievable."

Chad's face lit up. "Lucky," he said. "I love them."

"You do?" This piece of information surprised me in the best way possible.

"Yeah," he said.

"So who are we going to see tomorrow night?" I asked.

"Jugular Groove," he said. "It's my friend's band. They do an East meets West, jazz meets rock, fusion kind of thing."

Jenn raised her pretty little eyebrow. "You two are going out?"

I wanted to ignore her, but Chad seemed happy to answer—and looked happy when he said it. "Yeah. Tomorrow night."

The band sounded interesting. "Where are they playing?" I asked.

"The Dugout," Chad said.

"Okay," I replied. I'd never been there and had no idea where it was.

"Hello all!" Roland entered with his usual flourish. "Profiteroles, my favorite!"

"That's my line, Roland," I said, nudging him affectionately.

He smiled sweetly. "Forgive me, dear."

"Always," I said. "Now let's get to work."

We wrapped things up in the kitchen and went our separate ways. Chad seemed to want to linger, but so did Jenn, who won the pissing contest of who was going to get to talk to me alone.

"Lilah," said Chad. "Want to come by for dinner before the show?"

"That sounds great," I said.

He gave me his address and said, "Can we talk later tonight?"

"Sure," I said. "Call me in about an hour." After Chad left, I turned to Jenn, mightily annoyed. "What the fuck?" I said. "Don't you know when you're not wanted?"

"Chill," she said. "You'll have him all to yourself tomorrow night."

True, of course, but it still didn't excuse Jenn. "So what is it?"

Jenn put on her serious face. I rarely saw it, which was a good thing. I liked playful Jenn way better. "You seem mad at me," she said.

"Why on earth would I be mad at you?" I said. "Oh, wait, let's see, you took Richard's seat next to me at the concert, then you took Richard." I paused, and added for good measure, "Who happens to be my best friend's fiancé."

Jenn's little mouth opened into the cutest scoff I'd ever seen. "Right," she said. "And I'm sure you were just going to tuck him in and go home to get some rest. For Annemarie's sake."

I blushed. "That's not the point," I said.

"Why didn't you just come over? I thought you would."

"Really?"

She put her hands on her hips and looked at me with exasperation. "Duh."

"I thought you were trying to get rid of me," I said.

"When have I ever done that?" she asked, shaking her head.

"Lately," I said. "Since Iona's been around."

Jenn got quiet. "I'm sorry," she said. "Things with Iona are—different."

"Different than what?"

She got a faraway look in her eye. "Different than with anyone I've ever been with."

I adored Jenn, but I certainly wasn't in love with her, and the parameters of our relationship had been crystal clear from the get-go, so the stab of jealousy I felt didn't really make sense. "Lucky you," I said. It was meant to be sarcastic, but as the words came out of my mouth I realized I meant them. Then I remembered what she'd done and said coldly, "That didn't stop you from fucking Richard."

"Why would it?" she said. "We're poly, Lilah. Remember?"

"Doesn't mean I can't be jealous," I said. Ordinarily, I'd have been whispering that into her luscious ear, but there was the matter of my little celibacy pledge. Besides, I realized, shocking myself—I didn't want to.

Jenn cocked her head to the side and looked at me. "Something's going on," she said. "Is it Chad?"

I felt myself flush. "Don't be silly," I said.

Jenn laughed. "Okay, if that's the way you want to play it." I didn't know how I wanted to play it. I didn't understand my own feelings. "Hey," said Jenn. "Don't you want to hear about Richard?"

Thank goodness. A question for which I knew the answer. "Of course," I said. "Did he like Iona?"

"Iona's away until Saturday," said Jenn, looking very disappointed.

"Oh," I said. "You had him alone?" Jenn nodded, smiling wickedly. "Fun," she said, then her face registered a qualifier.

"But?" I said, prompting her. "But what?"

She frowned. It was cute. Everything Jenn did with her mouth was cute. "He couldn't stop talking about Annemarie."

"So?" I said. Jenn liked to listen to people's problems. She was better than any shrink I'd ever seen.

"It was just a little awkward," she said.

"Awkward?" That didn't make sense. As I tried to register what it meant, a flush bloomed in Jenn's cheeks. "Jenn, what are you talking about?"

"Annemarie came over the other night," she said. "Before Iona left town."

"And?" Jenn's face said it all, but I still couldn't believe it. "You fucked Annemarie?" I wasn't really asking her, just uttering a never-in-a-million-years-could-such-a-thing-happen kind of question. Jenn nodded, and I stood there in shock. It just couldn't be possible. "You've got to be kidding. You are kidding. Right?" Jenn shook her head, looking gleeful.

I didn't know how to feel about this piece of news. On top of the incredulity, there was more jealousy. And fear. What was happening to Annemarie, and why didn't I know about it? Why didn't she tell me? Was I not being there for her? Did I even know her? Did I ever know her?

My world was being rocked in more ways than one. I had to grab onto some kind of familiar territory. "I fucked Prado," I said, opting for bragging.

"In your dreams," said Jenn, bringing back her adorable scoff.

I pulled the tattered backstage pass from my bag. "Nope," I said. "In real, 3-D, Technicolor, surround sound life."

"Holy shit," said Jenn, then gave me a good shove. "And you're mad at me, you bitch!"

I laughed. "Come on, let's go for coffee and swap stories."

It was late, so we went to Jenn's place, where we wound up eating mounds of Vanilla Swiss Almond ice cream and talking into the wee hours. No sex, and no awkwardness. Jenn had excellent radar, and I think she knew it just wasn't the right thing.

We fell asleep a couple hours before sunrise, and I woke up exhausted, confused, but upon looking at Jenn slumbering peacefully next to me—happy. She was an excellent friend, and I was grateful.

I snuck out quietly, leaving Jenn a thank you note, and went home, where I made a beeline for my bedroom to sleep another few hours. I wanted to be rested for my big date with Chad. Before putting on my eye mask, I checked my phone and realized that I had completely forgotten the conversation Chad wanted to have with me the night before. To his credit, he'd only called once, but he had left a message. Shit, I thought, dialing my voice mail.

*Hey. Sorry you're not there. Call me when you can.*

That was it. I supposed I had to call him before showing up at his house for dinner. I dialed and he picked up on the third ring. "Hi," he said.

I realized I'd never talked with him on the phone before. He had a really nice voice, which helped calm my nerves. "Hi," I said. "I'm looking forward to tonight."

"Great," he said. "Me, too." Awkward silence came next, but I wasn't going to break it. He was the one who wanted the conversation. "I just wanted to check in about what happened the other night."

"What do you mean?" I asked.

"You left so abruptly," he said. "Why?"

"I told you, I needed to get to work early the next day."

"Lilah," he whispered. "Let's not start things off this way."

"What way?"

"You know what I mean."

"I'm sorry," I said. "When you didn't want go upstairs, I figured you didn't like me." It was still a lie, but I realized to my own surprise that it wasn't a total lie.

"Not the case," he said. "Not at all."

"I'm glad," I said.

Chad paused, then took a sharp intake of breath before asking, "What's up with you and Jenn?"

These were mighty personal questions before we'd even had an official date. "We're friends," I said.

"Sorry," he said. "I'm not trying to be nosy. I just want to understand."

"Okay," I said. "Let's talk more tonight."

Chad agreed and we hung up, me wondering what the heck I was getting myself into. I really liked Chad, and I really wanted Chad, but I hoped the third degree was going to stop soon.

After my nap, I took a long shower and headed to the closet to figure out what to wear. I hadn't felt such delicious anticipation about a date in a very long time. Most surprising of all, it had nothing to do with sex, because I intended to keep my celibacy pledge. I felt like a teenager and briefly wondered whether I was evolving or devolving. Before I could give that a second thought (not that I was going to), Annemarie came storming in.

"Hey," she said, heading straight for her bedroom.

I followed her, and tried to make like Chad and demand an explanation for why she was packing her overnight bag with sexy lingerie, but she wasn't about to tell me. I didn't let on that I knew about Jenn and Iona, either. There was no way she was spending the weekend with them, anyway — Iona wouldn't even be back until Saturday and Jenn wouldn't leave town without her.

Something else was up, but I didn't like that Annemarie wasn't leveling with me. I couldn't spend much time dwelling on it, though, Chad was expecting me in half an hour. As I was walking out the door, who should call but Richard?

"Lilah," he said when I answered. I had thought maybe he and Annemarie patched things up, and she really was going away with him, and they were calling to let me know everything was back to normal. As soon as I heard Richard's urgent, desperate, and scared voice I knew that wasn't the case.

I might have chewed him out for having ditched me and gone home with Jenn, but I was in too good of a mood, and besides, he was in trouble. "Hey," I said gently.

"Where's Annemarie?"

"I don't know."

"She went away for the weekend."

"How do you know?"

"Carol told me." Annemarie wouldn't be happy about that. "Where did she go?"

"I don't know," I said again.

"Come on, Lilah. Don't hold out on me."

He was sounding more aggressive, and I was feeling less sympathetic. "I told you I don't know where she is," I said.

"You expect me to believe that?"

"Believe it or not," I said. "I don't care. She texted me and said she'd be back Sunday or Monday. That's all I know."

"Monday?" He practically wailed it. "Where could she be?"

"No clue," I said. "Really."

"What if she's not okay?"

I guffawed. "I think she's fine," I said.

"Why do you think that?"

"I just do."

"Lilah, come on. Talk to me."

"I don't have anything to say," I said. "I really do think she's okay." Richard was silent on the other end of the phone "Try not to worry." More silence. "You could go see Jenn," I said icily.

Richard must have really been in a bad way, because he ignored that. "If you hear from her," he said, sounding defeated, "tell her I called."

The whole world was going crazy. I included myself in that assessment, but maybe it was in a good way. That's how it felt at the moment, at least, as I thought about my upcoming evening. I headed out the door to Chad's.

Chad's apartment was just outside the city—not in suburbia, but in the college town next door on the second floor of a multi-family house.

I rarely ventured away from my busy urban neighborhood, and while Chad (thank goodness) didn't live in an environment that resembled country life, it was the quietest place I'd been in for awhile.

I rang the doorbell that said *Chad Snow*. Almost immediately, I heard footsteps coming down the stairs, then the door opened and he was standing there, looking amazing.

"Hi," he said, smiling. He was wearing his denim cut-offs again, with a hunter green tank top that showed off his shoulders and biceps. They were nicely conditioned, and artfully tattooed, another nice surprise. "Come on in," he said, moving his brown locks away from his beautiful brown eyes with a toss of his head.

I followed him up the stairs, enjoying the view of his ass immensely, and wondering whether there was any hope of not breaking my celibacy pledge.

The top of the stairs opened into Chad's living room, which, by city standards, was downright spacious. There was an old couch covered with a paisley slipcover in the corner, a couple of chairs, and a coffee table with books and magazines all over it. Woven area rugs were scattered on the floorboards in appropriate places, and there was even a fireplace.

As a baker, I was attuned to smells, and something smelled delicious. Besides what was cooking in the kitchen, Chad's apartment had an earthy, inviting odor I couldn't quite place. My eyes fell on a large, exquisite cabinet against the far wall, and it hit me. Wood. The place smelled of wood. I remembered Chad's e-mail address—*Woodworker777*—and started putting two and two together. "Did you make that?" I asked, pointing to the cabinet.

"Yeah," he said. "That's my other job."

I looked at the coffee table again, and saw that it was beautifully crafted, with an engraved solid wood top and steel supports. "That, too?"

"Yup," said Chad. "It's all recycled. That tree fell in my parents' backyard."

"Wow," I said. "What else did you make from it?"

Chad shrugged. "A night table," he said. "A bunch of cutting boards."

"Really?" I said, interested. "Do you work here?"

"Studio's in the basement," he said. "Are you hungry?"

"Famished," I said, smiling.

"Good," he said. "Everything's just about ready."

I focused on the smells wafting in from the kitchen. "Steak?" I said. "I love steak."

"I know," he said. "Medium rare."

"How do you know?" I asked, running various stalking scenarios through my mind.

"We talk about food in the kitchen a lot," Chad said. "You mentioned it."

Of course. I liked to talk about food. It was part of my sensual persona. I honed my nose in more sharply. "Fennel," I said. I couldn't place anything else.

Chad nodded and started walking into the kitchen, which turned out to be huge. Sliding doors opened onto a deck, where the grill was. The steak was steaming on the table, next to a gorgeous green salad sprinkled with what looked like honeyed almonds, currants, strawberries, and avocado. "Milady," said Chad, pulling out a chair that he might have actually made himself.

"Why thank you," I said, enjoying the chivalry. The steak shimmered on my plate. It was smothered with a salty, peppery fennel rub and cooked to a juicy brown, the fatty edges crisp and blackened. Sweet of Chad to make something he knew I liked. What he may not have thought about was that it was a considerable risk. Getting a steak right was hard.

Oh well, I told myself as Chad poured me a glass of red wine. Eating a perfect steak is a rare occurrence. I couldn't hold it against Chad if his weren't impeccable.

"Dig in," he said, smiling.

I cut into the meat, which took barely any effort it was so tender and so perfectly pink. Chad watched as I pierced a hunk with my fork and put it in my mouth. He seemed to be enjoying looking at me, and not at all nervous, which was nice. It relieved me of feeling any awkwardness or pressure about responding to his cooking, which turned out to be—well, perfect.

"Oh my god," I said as the steak melted in my mouth, releasing delectable bursts of salty fennel and just a trace of kick. "This is amazing."

Chad cut his own steak and started eating. "Thanks," he said. "I learned it from the chef at the restaurant where I was waiting tables in college."

"You sure did," I said, savoring the flavor and the hotness on my tongue. "Cayenne?" I asked.

"That was the hardest part," he said. "Getting just the right amount."

I nodded. "Tell me about it," I said. "It took a lot of experimenting to master my peppery dinner rolls."

"Dinner rolls?" he said.

"Yeah," I said, taking a bite of salad. "Before the hotel, I worked at a New York bakery. We made a lot of bread and rolls."

"Oh," he said. "I want you to make those for me sometime."

I hadn't made bread in years, but the thought of doing it with Chad, in his large and very well-stocked kitchen, gave me a hankering for it. "I'd love to," I said.

Chad smiled, blowing his hair out of his eyes so I could see them. They were shining. At me.

Did it make my pussy warm? Yes, it did. But it made my heart, the neglect of which each passing second revealed ever more blatantly, even warmer.

I kept my pledge. It was no trouble. There were so many other things to enjoy.

The food, of course. And the wine. The chocolate mousse that Chad made, which also had a hint of cayenne. He liked things hot.

The weather was obliging on that score. It was in the 90's again, and humid, with no break in sight. That made us both very sweaty, which neither of us seemed to mind. Working in kitchens, I was used to heat, and I was glad that Chad's tastes ran hot, and hoped that he'd prove fiery in the bedroom, too. Eventually, of course, eventually.

My sundress stuck to me like glue, and I thought Chad liked that, because I caught him looking quite a few times. I smiled at him, letting him know I saw, and he seemed to feel no embarrassment. Having my body admired without the inevitability of subsequent fucking was, if not novel, a blast from the past. It was different as a grown-up, though, more comfortable, and a lot more fun.

The music was weird, but I liked it a lot, and I especially liked the butchy drummer who reminded me a little bit of Iona. My mind started to run to the usual place, probably out of habit, but to my astonishment the fantasy fell flat before it ever got going. Instead, I found myself looking at Chad, liking his attention to and appreciation of the music.

After the band played two sets, we walked back to Chad's place, where my car was parked, and talked. Thankfully, he didn't bring up Jenn or any other concerns he might have had about me ditching him at Rialto's.

Chad had introduced me to his friend, who played sax and whose name was Grant. He'd introduced me to the drummer, whose name was Lee and who was very personable, which I'd managed to notice since when I shook her hand the thought of sex didn't even enter my mind.

Instead, I was filled with excitement. This night had been so different. Chad's congested but homey neighborhood, stuffed with densely packed triple deckers and trees and grass. The dinner he'd so painstakingly prepared. The edgy live music in the hole in the wall club. But most of all Chad, smart, sweet, and full-of-surprises Chad.

He held my hand as we walked, and it felt so good. How many years had it been since I'd had my hand held on a date without the tension of sex to follow? The late night air had cooled down a bit, and I breathed it deeply. It felt fresh and new, the way Chad felt.

When we got to my car, he turned to me. "I had a really great time," he said, locking his brown eyes onto mine.

"Me, too," I said, and for some inexplicable reason, I wanted to cry.

As though reading my thoughts, Chad cradled my cheek and gently brushed underneath my eye with his thumb. Every part of me—my pussy, my tits, my arms, legs, back, and stomach—tingled.

Chad's face leaned closer to mine, and I knew he was going to kiss me. It was a comfortable, unhurried knowledge. His lips moved toward mine in what felt like delicious slow motion, smells of wine and chocolate and sweat, his sweet Chad breath, the flesh of his lips touching mine ever so slightly, then more, pressing and parting.

I closed my eyes and opened to the kiss, a warm sea of wetness and tongues, a perfect union of smoothness and suction and moistness.

It ended as it had begun, only in reverse, and we both stood motionless for awhile after it was over, our foreheads touching, our quickened breath mingling.

"Good night," he finally whispered, retreating. He took the car keys from my hand and clicked the keyless entry, then went around and opened the door for me.

I climbed inside and said good night back, and he kissed me one more time, quickly, on the lips, and I drove home in a deliriously delicious daze.

# Chapter 17

# Home Again

**ANNEMARIE**

Except for one long, luxurious hike up the mountain by the cottage, we stayed indoors for the entire weekend. The refrigerator was well stocked — apparently Zach had put in an order with the local delivery service earlier in the week.

"Before you knew I was coming?" I teased as we sat at the kitchen table, enjoying the best lamb chops I'd ever eaten. "Wasn't that a little presumptuous?"

"I wanted to be prepared," he said. "Just in case. Mmmm, these are good, if I do say so myself."

"You're an excellent cook," I said, letting the tender meat melt in my mouth. It wasn't idle flattery. We'd already had scrumptious eggs Benedict for breakfast, and arugula salad with goat cheese and a divine sweet, mustardy dressing for lunch. I sampled a bit of the risotto he'd made to go with the lamb. "Wow," I said. "What did you put in this?"

"Love," he said. "My secret ingredient." I laughed, slightly nervously. That was a big word to be using during our first weekend together. "Annemarie?" he said inquiringly.

"Yes?" I replied, looking at my plate.

"It's just an expression." Really, he could read me like a book. "I do care for you, though." He reached across the table and slipped his hand into mine. "A lot."

I cared for him a lot, too, but there were times during the weekend when waves of panic took my breath away, and I had to close my eyes, count to ten, and practice more self-talk than I'd needed in year. The feelings I was having were not what I expected to be experiencing weeks before I was scheduled to marry another man. Nothing in my carefully constructed life seemed to be following a conventional, or planned, trajectory at the moment. Contrary to what seemed to make logical sense, my new feelings for Zach didn't obliterate my feelings for Richard. Rather, they resided with them, and each seemed to feed the other. It was mysterious, and terrifying, but I tried to recall what Zach said about our hearts and their capability for love. I was beginning to believe it. I wondered whether Richard would see it that way.

Zach dropped me off in front of my building early on Sunday evening with a long, delicious, farewell kiss and a promise to call in the next few days. I watched as he drove away, heading for the airport to go home, then I turned to the front door. The night was hot, much hotter than it had been in New Hampshire. The heatwave hadn't yet broken, and the air was thick and steamy and still.

Whether or not that was the only thing causing my hesitation, I didn't feel ready to go home just yet. Besides being a fabulous lover, Zach had proved to be a great listener, and weird as it seemed, he'd helped me sort through what I had to say to Richard. I was scared about the encounter, but it couldn't be delayed. As much as I needed to know what was going to happen with us, though, was something else I needed to know first. I looked at my phone, at the text from Jenn I'd read in the car.

*Free tonight?*

It had come in early that afternoon, short and sweet, but the invitation was clear. I hadn't answered it, or any of the many texts and messages that piled up over the weekend, from Richard, From Lilah, from Carol, and from my mother, who was certainly calling about the wedding. I'd have to face all of them soon, very soon, but now that Zach and I had finally made love and forged what felt like a deep connection, I had to see how it would feel to be with Jenn and Iona again, to try and clear up the loose ends about what exactly I wanted for myself and for my life, before I talked to Richard.

I decided to walk, since Jenn didn't live far from us and would probably think sweaty was sexy (I had to admit, my newly evolved sexuality was leaning in that direction, too). When I got to her building, an older lady with a couple of bags from the twenty four hour store was opening the front door with her key. She smiled at me and held the door so I could go inside. I entered the building, nodded to thank her, and took the stairs to Jenn's apartment.

She answered right after I knocked, but instead of the smile I expected to see on her face, there was a look of shocked surprise. "Hey," I said, smiling, "The answer is yes. I'm free tonight."

Jenn stood there speechless, her mouth opened into that cute little button it made. She wore a thin, silky bathrobe that wasn't tied as tightly as it should have been, at least if she didn't want to reveal the fact that underneath it she was stark naked. I was about to ask whether she was going to invite me in, when a familiar voice called from inside. It came from Jenn's bedroom. "Jenn," it said. "Let me give you some money."

The strangest thing happened next. Richard stepped out of Jenn's bedroom, into view, while another man holding a brown paper bag stepped off the elevator and into the hallway.

I saw Richard at the exact moment I smelled what was unmistakably Chef Wong's General Gao's Chicken. After all, Richard and I had used the twenty four hour delivery service enough times for me to know it anywhere. Richard wore nothing but a pair of black silk boxers—boxers which I had given him—and he held a twenty dollar bill.

He stopped cold when he saw me, and there we were, all shocked, all completely frozen, except for the delivery man, who recognized me immediately and bowed his head in acknowledgement. "How do you do, Ms. Fitch?"

I didn't want him to see Jenn and Richard half-dressed, so I blocked the doorway and summoned my nerves of steel. "Very well, thank you, Fred," I answered while rummaging through my purse and pulling out enough money for the food and a generous tip.

When I was done and Fred was safely in the elevator, I handed the bag to Jenn, who was still standing frozen in the doorway, looking scared. Richard had disappeared. "Here," I said. "I'm sorry I disturbed you."

I turned to leave and had only taken a few steps when I heard Richard coming after me. "Annemarie," he said. "Wait."

So many conflicting feelings coursed through me—relief and satisfaction that he was chasing me, anger at the reckless chances he was taking with our future, confusion about being so mad because of what I had been doing myself, and above and beyond everything else, mind-numbing jealousy.

I didn't slow down. I knew Richard would catch up to me, and he did, the instant I entered the stairwell. "Annemarie, please," he said. He'd gotten dressed—denim cut-offs and his Eats T-shirt with the Teva sandals he should have gotten rid of a long time ago but loved too much to throw away.

"Please, what?" I said icily, sarcastically, angrily.

"Talk to me," he said, practically whispering. "Please, just talk to me."

His voice sounded so exposed, and so vulnerable, and so real, so much like when we first courted and fell in love. What had happened since? Time passing. Familiarity. And, of course, my climb up the hotel ladder, my carefully constructed persona, my calling the shots about our relationship. How did so many barriers get between us?

I saw the fear in Richard's face, and felt it reflect back at me, and I knew the answer. As terrified as Richard was, he could never be as scared as I had been and still was. In fact, he'd been the brave one, brave enough to push the envelope, to let go and let us grow.

I had to talk to him, and I wanted to, but this wasn't what I'd had in mind. I told myself to forget all that. Maybe, just maybe, I could take a deep enough breath to go with the flow and let it happen. "Your hair," I said, reaching out and touching Richard's unruly mop. "It's a mess."

He grabbed onto my hand and squeezed. "Not as big of a mess as I am," he said, pulling me to him suddenly and hugging me almost tighter than I could bear. "I love you," he said, his face buried in my neck.

I felt his hot tears wetting my already hot, clammy skin, but I didn't let go. I was crying myself, and in need of someone to hold onto.

I don't know how long we stood there holding each other. Long enough. Then I said, "Let's go talk," and we walked out of Jenn's building, into the hot, hot night.

We went back to Richard's place, even though it was a bit of a drive. He had his car, and I didn't want to chance running into anyone, even Lilah.

He flicked on the light as we walked into the kitchen and I did a double take. "Jesus," I said. "You like your surroundings to reflect your inner turmoil, huh?"

Richard smiled wryly. "It's not calculated," he said.

"How many days' worth of dishes is that?" I asked, pointing to the stacks of plates, cups, and empty take-out containers on the counter.

"I don't know," Richard shrugged. "Lost count." He ran his fingers through his hair, closed his eyes, and sighed deeply. "I'm glad you're here, Annemarie."

"So am I," I said with conviction. Even the disgusting mess couldn't distract me from that truth.

"Let's sit down," said Richard, heading for the living room.

"Coming," I said, stopping to get myself a glass of water. I was parched, like I'd spent the day in a desert.

I filled one for Richard, too, threw some ice cubes into the glasses, and joined him on the couch. He smiled as I handed him his water, and we both drank. "Annemarie," he said, and laughed nervously. "I just want to keep saying your name." He paused. "I don't know what else to say."

"Maybe you could start by telling me what you were doing with Jenn." Wow. Back home, back with Richard, and bossy Annemarie was springing right into action. If old habits die hard, old relationship patterns die even harder. Richard turned a bright shade of red and opened his mouth to speak, but no words came out. I put my hand on his and softened my voice. "It's okay," I said. "We don't have to start there."

That opened the flood gates. Richard confessed everything–that he'd been thinking about polyamory for awhile but hadn't known how to bring it up with me. "Is this Lilah's doing?" I asked. Despite the pleasure I'd taken in my recent adventures, part of me was still thinking about what my life had been just a short time ago, and how it might have sped forward according to my plan if not for Richard's intervention.

"No," he said. "Not really." He paused. "Partly maybe. I mean, watching her lifestyle, and seeing how well it could work."

"I don't know about that," I said, because despite all of her shenanigans, I'd always considered Lilah to be unhappy.

We stayed silent for a few moments, then Richard put his arm around me and pulled me to him. "But it could work," he said. "For us."

He phrased it as though he were asking a question, a rhetorical question maybe, but I answered it. "Yes," I said. "I think it could."

I felt his body stiffen in surprise, then let go. "Annemarie," he whispered. "Where did you go this weekend?"

I took a big deep breath, and dove headfirst into the waters.

The conversation went long into the night and was probably the hardest conversation I'd ever had. It was different than addressing the subject with Zach had been, because Zach, as much as I adored him (and Joanne, too), would only ever be a secondary. Richard was the man to whom I was betrothed, the man with whom I wanted to spend my life, however we worked that out.

Although I hadn't gone behind his back with Jenn and Zach, or so I'd told myself given the circumstances, I still felt a pang of guilt as I told Richard the story. First, Jenn, and that elicited a good bit of surprise, and some delight. "Details?" he asked timidly, and a little mischievously.

"Maybe later," I said, ignoring his playfulness. We had to get through this business before any real fun could be had. I plowed ahead and told him about Zach. "I spent the weekend with a man," I said.

"Oh," whispered Richard, a pained look on his face. "And you—had sex?" I looked down when I felt myself blush. It wasn't easy to talk about your sex life with your fiancé. In fact, it was terrifying. "Oh, Annemarie."

I felt terrible. I didn't want to hurt him, even though he'd hurt me, but what did I think? Hurt was inevitable with this lifestyle, wasn't it? The memory of seeing Jenn and Richard together popped into my mind. It stung, but I wasn't in a position to be mad at Richard. If I'd learned one thing through all this, it was that blaming was pointless, because the source of the pain never came from only one place.

I turned to Richard, who turned away. "Look at me," I said, putting two fingers on his chin and gently pulling his face. Our eyes met, and there was no barrier between us now. "This is what you wanted, isn't it?"

"In theory," he said. "Reality is harder."

"Yes," I answered, tearing up. "But it has more to offer." Richard smiled tentatively, but said nothing. A thought came to my mind, something I'd been thinking about for the last few days. "Did you," I asked, praying he had the right answer. "With Lilah?"

"No," he said, shaking his head. "No."

"But you want to."

He hesitated, and I could see the *no* forming on his lips, but he stopped before saying it. "It's occurred to me," he said. "But you're more important."

"Thank you," I said. "For not doing that."

He grabbed me and hugged me hard again. "Can we do this, Annemarie? Jesus, the thought of you with another man is killing me."

"Man?" I said. "What about Jenn?"

He laughed. "That doesn't bother me as much for some reason."

I smiled wryly. The reason was obvious, and I didn't like it, but the raging jealousy I felt when I thought about Richard and Jenn made it clear I wasn't immune to ingrained social messages, either. "We'll have to talk more, figure out what we're comfortable with, what works for us." Richard nodded and hugged me, burying his face in my shirt. "No more sex with other people until we do." I felt a wet spot on my shoulder that was more than just humidity-induced sweat. "Richard," I pulled away and looked at his glassy eyes.

"I was so scared," he whispered.

"Me, too," I said.

"We're okay?" he asked, his face edging closer to mine.

A wave of relief flooded through me. Whatever happened, whatever we decided, Richard was my priority. "We're fantastic," I said, feeling his breath on my face and a clenching between my legs.

He kissed me, a long, wet kiss that seemed to last and last and last. After the tender slowness of that, an urgency overcame us both and without any more words, we ripped off our clothes and entwined our naked bodies.

I reclined on the couch and opened my legs, and Richard was inside me. His entry flooded me with the biggest sense of relief I'd ever felt, and one thought came clearly and joyfully into my mind—home.

*This. Is. Home.*

The words played in my mind like a mantra, exploding with giddy certainty as Richard and I came, together.

# Chapter 18
# Feels Like the First Time

**LILAH**

I slept well after my date with Chad, better than I had in awhile, a better sleep than any valerian or sleep balm or lavender-tinged eye mask could have provided. On Saturday, I woke feeling peaceful.

The heatwave was still in full force, but the early morning hour provided a little relief from the high temperatures. I stretched out lazily in my bed and heard my phone vibrate.

*Good Morning* said the little bubble that popped onto my screen.

It was Chad, with his uncanny ability (or luck, my cynical side tried to point out) to perceive my every move. I pictured his face saying it, his eyes slightly obscured by his hair, his mouth smiling gently. I texted him back. *Same to you.*

*Off to the kitchen?*

*Of course.*

*I'm working, too.*

I knew he wasn't on the schedule until Tuesday, so he must have meant that he was working at home. I pictured him there, his biceps flexing as he fashioned a hunk of oak into something beautiful, his sweet, woody smell pervading the air. *What are you making?*

*Bookshelves.*

*I'm making eclairs, croissants, and fruit tarts.*

*Sounds like fun.*

*Not as much fun without you.* :)

I would be working into the wee hours again, but we decided we'd actually talk when I got home from my shift. What I really wanted was to see him again, and the fact that he hadn't brought that up in our communication was a little concerning. I was relieved that on our date he hadn't brought up the Rialto's debacle, or Jenn, but I had a sinking feeling they might be coming home to roost.

*Call me when you get in,* Chad texted. *Doesn't matter what time.*

*Will do,* I replied. *Can't wait.* It was mostly true.

Jenn and Roland were on the weekend schedule, and we had a lot of fun. Roland was in a fine mood, singing show tunes in his impressive baritone while whipping up cream filling for the eclairs.

He was also sweating a lot. "Hey you," I said. "Be careful or that filling is going to be way too salty."

Roland laughed and wiped his brow with a towel. "Never fear, Madame Lilah," he said. "No dripping into the bowl! It will not happen!" We all cracked up. Roland was the kind of guy who could be funny saying things that wouldn't have been a bit humorous out of someone else's mouth. He expertly separated several eggs and dropped the yolks into a bowl while belting out *I Could Have Danced All Night.*

The rest of the shift went much the same. When it was over, Jenn asked if I wanted to come by for one of her coconut milk smoothies, but I declined. "Plans?" she asked with a wink.

"Yes," I answered, feeling a bit of dread about the prospect of a serious conversation with Chad.

When I got home, I took off all my clothes and dropped into bed before dialing his number. He picked up immediately. "Hey," he said.

"Hey," I answered.

"You sound happy."

"I am," I said.

"And you didn't even make profiteroles today," he teased.

I laughed. "Croissants are almost as much fun because they're such a challenge."

"You like a challenge, don't you?" His voice dropped low. There was mischief in it.

"Sometimes," I said. "What about you? How are the bookshelves?"

"Finished," he said. "They just need to be stained. I also started on a chess set and some bunk beds."

"Wow," I said. "Productive."

"Yeah," he said. "I also finished *Anna Karenina*."

"Oh," I said. "Was it sad?"

"Of course. But more than that."

"How so?"

"Levin finally finds spiritual fulfillment."

"You mean he gets religion?"

"Not exactly." I didn't answer, because I didn't really want to talk about *Anna Karenina*.

An awkward pause ensued, then Chad said. "I had a good time last night."

It should have been a nice thing to hear, but I sensed a qualifier. I chose, however, to ignore it. "Me, too," I said, with as sexy a voice as I could muster.

Chad wasn't having it. "I wish we were having this conversation in person," he said.

"Why don't we?" I answered. "I'm free."

"Now?"

"Yes," I said. "You come here. Now."

In the 20 minutes it took Chad to get to my apartment, I took a cool shower, changed my sheets, and frantically tidied up my bedroom. I was glad Annemarie wasn't around to distract me with questions or comments. I wanted all my attention on Chad.

Not that it was difficult to achieve that. The sound of the doorbell sent a wave of excitement — or was it nerves — through me.

It seemed to take forever for Chad to get up to our floor. My heart was pounding and my stomach did somersaults the whole time. When I heard the whoosh of the elevator door opening, I wiped my sweaty palms on the black silk nightie I'd chosen after going through my closet and realizing I didn't need to wear actual clothes. I'd even decided to forego undergarments, and my bare pussy clenching and moistening when I laid eyes on Chad felt delicious, and distracted from my less pleasant feelings of fear.

"You look amazing," he said, taking me into his arms for a long, slow hug. I couldn't squeeze him tightly enough. I felt greedy, every second wanting more of him.

"Ditto," I whispered when we finally pulled away from each other and I gave Chad a once over. He was only wearing baggy cargo shorts and flip flops, but his yellow tank top was skimpy enough to show his strong tattooed arms, and tight enough to show his amazing pecs and washboard stomach underneath.

The thought of that thrilled me. I loved a guy who was ripped, and the sight of Chad brought my old lusty animal self to the forefront. It felt good to have it back, but it wasn't alone. It was joined by the more unfamiliar, emotionally vulnerable Lilah who, realizing she cared way too much about the outcome of this encounter, suddenly freaked out.

A chill wrenched my gut and it felt like a wall came down inside me, blocking and smothering what I'd been so lately and so happily rediscovering. I turned and headed for the couch, where I sat down and took one of those giant cleansing breaths that always worked, even for Annemarie, or so she told me after Stephanie of the awesome yoga classes taught her how to do it.

Chad sat next to me, putting his arm around me. "Tell me," he said.

"Tell you what?"

"Tell me what's going on."

"What makes you think something's going on?" He tossed his hair out of his eyes with that gesture I loved so much, and he smiled, not saying a word. He was simply waiting, with more patience than I could ever muster in a million years. My heart was pounding as I spoke. I was terrified. "Chad, you know I'm bisexual, right?"

He stroked my hair, my cheek, my chin. "I figured something like that."

"Why?" I asked.

"You and Jenn," he said. "It's pretty obvious."

I found myself blushing. "There's nothing serious between us," I said. "Except our friendship."

"Good," he whispered.

"Why good?"

"Because I want to be serious with you." I was still scared, but at that statement from Chad I wanted to jump for joy. I felt hot. I really, really wanted to fuck Chad and I knew that any celibacy pledge I'd made to myself was going out the window fast, but something was different. I didn't feel like I did before fucking Jenn or the bartender at Rialto's or Prado and Sue. It had been years since I'd cared a whole lot what would happen after the fact, but with Chad, I cared very much. "Lilah," said Chad. "Why did you really take off that night at Rialto's?"

"I don't know," I lied.

"Sorry," he said, stiffening. "You'll have to do better than that."

I took a deep breath. "I wanted to have sex and you didn't," I said.

He nodded as though he'd known it all along. "Is sex still all you want from me?"

"Absolutely not. It's not all I wanted then, either." I paused. "I think we might have different viewpoints on sex."

Chad looked at me. I had an inkling he might be having a hard time with the conversation, but he wasn't avoiding it. "What do you mean by that?"

I wiped my sweaty palms on my silky nightgown and took a deep breath. "I'm not just bi," I said. "I'm polyamorous."

Chad flinched ever so slightly. At least I thought he did. I couldn't be sure because as quickly as it might have happened, it was gone. "What does that mean?"

"It means I'm not monogamous." Chad stayed silent. Thankfully, he never took his eyes from mine. He didn't turn away, at least. That was something. "Can you deal with that?" I asked.

"I don't know," he said. He was leaning imperceptibly closer to me with each passing minute, or else I was imagining it, or else I was the one edging my face toward his. Really, it felt more like there was a gigantic magnetic field between us that wasn't going to stop until our bodies were glued against each other.

"The funny thing is," I whispered, "lately I don't want to be with anyone but you."

"That's good," he said. I felt his breath brush my face like a warm, moist feather.

"Why good?"

"Because I want you," he said. "And I'm not gonna lie. I want you all to myself." My eyes welled up with tears. When was the last time someone wanted only me? You know it's not going to last, my cynical, or perhaps realistic, voice warned. "It's okay," Chad said, his lips so close to mine now.

"What if it changes? What if you change, or I change?"

"We'll worry about that if it happens," he whispered in my ear, licking the studs along the edge of it, making my insides zing. "Right now, let's worry about this." He kissed me, the same long, slow, deep kiss he'd given me the night before, but more urgent, filled with readiness and desire.

I kissed him back, hungry and hard, and felt his hands rub my breasts through the silky black fabric of my nightgown. My nipples hardened under his touch. I moaned, he squeezed, my pussy gave a little gush.

"Let me," I said, pushing him away and tearing off my nightgown, and heading for my bedroom where already, candles were lit and the sheets were turned down. I lay on my side on the futon, propped up on my elbow as I watched Chad take off his clothes.

There was the amazing hairless chest, the rippled abdomen underneath, and the biggest prize of all, his erect cock. I liked a big rod, and Chad's didn't disappoint.

I scooted over to give him room on the bed, and he lay beside me, also on his side, face to face so we were yet again looking into each other's eyes. "Lilah," he whispered.

"Yes?" I said.

"I like saying your name." He kissed me again, passionately, gently pushing me onto my back and pressing his naked body onto mine.

"Jesus, Chad," I cried, overwhelmed by the feel of his skin on mine. I could stay glued to him forever, just like this, I thought, but he had other ideas. He rolled back on his side and played with my nipples, this time with no silk barrier, and I moaned with pleasure.

"Do you know how long I've wanted to fuck you?" he whispered. He leaned over and licked my erect nipples, then drew one into his mouth and sucked it, which sent me out of my mind, much too out of my mind to answer. "You like this?" he asked, still sucking. I moaned, and hoped it was answer enough. He stopped sucking and ran his fingers along my arms, my thighs, my belly. Any lighter would have tickled, any harder would have been too much, but Chad's touch was perfect. I thought of my big white feather and let out another deep moan. Chad leaned into my ear and whispered, "Are you wet?"

"Oh, yes," I said. The words came unbidden to my lips, as natural as breathing. "So. Fucking. Wet."

Chad was up on his knees. "Let me see," he said, drawing my knees apart, spreading me open. He looked at my pussy like it was the most priceless jewel on the planet. *Bless you, Chad,* I thought. Bless the man who can make me feel so hot and so special all at the same time.

"Mmmm," he said, appreciatively. His fingers brushed my lips and I shivered. Chad slipped one inside me, his thumb pressing gently on my nub, and I thought I'd come right then and there. Before I could, he withdrew his hand and just looked at my pussy again, his hands resting gently on the inside of my thighs.

I looked at him kneeling over me, his gorgeous cock jutting out over his balls. I wanted that cock, and those balls. I wanted to hold them, lick them, suck them, fuck them. "I love your cock," I said, but there was no answer. Chad was too busy diving into the supplies I'd left on the night table, tearing open a dental dam and placing it on my pussy. The instant his tongue touched me I came, bucking gratefully into his face.

As I lay there panting, he grabbed my ass cheeks from underneath and squeezed, never taking his mouth from my pussy. Once I settled down he started licking me softly, one finger slipping into me, rubbing and gyrating gently. I felt another wave building, and as it grew, Chad worked me harder, drawing my nub into his mouth and sucking, finding that oh so sweet spot inside me. "Do it, baby," he whispered, and I knew just what he meant, and I knew that I would.

The wave built, tapping the deepest, fullest wells inside me. I felt myself expand until I burst, hot, clear liquid spilling all over the clean sheets. My deeply relaxed body went limp. Chad kissed my pussy gently, then my belly, my rib cage, my breasts, neck, and lips. "You're so beautiful, Lilah," he whispered, and I felt again how much his words thrilled me.

He hugged me tight, and as each second passed, I felt the bond between us grow. I also felt his hard cock pressing into my thigh. I kissed his ear, letting my hot breath stream softly into it. He moaned as I started working my way down, working his body and his skin with my mouth, getting closer to that beautiful rod, around and around and around it but not touching it, not with my hands or my mouth, until I knew he was going crazy. "Lilah," he cried. "Please."

I rolled a condom onto it and kissed the tip, swirling my tongue around the silky head, then down the wrinkly shaft, then licking the damp, soft balls, before taking him full in my mouth. I sucked him with reverence and concentration, enjoying every second of it.

When I knew he was close to coming, I stopped and kissed his mouth, whispering his name like a mantra. I climbed over him, mounting him, claiming him. Our eyes were locked onto each other as I lowered my pussy onto his cock, slowly, surely, feeling every inch of him penetrate me, until he was fully inside me, my clit pressed against him.

I lifted myself slowly and lowered myself onto him again, faster and harder this time, and the instant my clit made contact with his skin, the moment his cock hit the deepest part of me, we exploded and cried out together. Chad grabbed onto me and we held each other tight, and I didn't even try to hold back the flood of tears that overcame me.

# Chapter 19
# Wedding Bells

## LILAH

I'd had a lot of sex in my life before Chad, but I'd never had sex like I had with Chad. I didn't know what that meant. That he was a monumental piece of ass? That a period of celibacy (however short) made fucking that much better? That I was in love?

I suppose the last option was a possibility, but not one I was eager to entertain too consciously. I didn't want to scare myself off, after all. Really, I wanted to fuck Chad again, and it looked like it wouldn't be long before that would happen — four days, to be precise, until our next date.

In the meantime, we were spending a lot of time on the phone. We had serious talks, about books and movies, about what we wanted out of life, even about politics, which thankfully we agreed on. We also had playful talks, and for those, I had plenty of toys. Besides being a better real time lay than anyone I'd had the pleasure of bedding, Chad was also the best virtual lay. Phone sex never felt so good.

I was on Cloud Nine, flying so high that I hadn't given much of a thought to Annemarie, or Richard, who'd left three messages and more texts than I could count on my phone over the weekend. I knew something big was going on with Annemarie, but I imagined that she was unraveling, not thriving, so when she walked in on Monday night glowing brighter than Sirius, I was surprised. "Lilah," she said, embracing me. Even her hug felt different. Longer than usual, and closer.

"Hey, you," I said, releasing the hug and holding her at arm's length. She looked more beautiful than I'd ever seen her look, which was saying something. "Where have you been?"

144

Annemarie smiled. "Around the world and back again."

"Oh?" I said. "And I thought you only went to New Hampshire."

"Come on, let's get something to drink," she said, kicking off her sandals, opening the fridge, and removing a jug of my special home made lemonade. "Perfect," she said, pouring two glasses.

"Thanks," I said, taking a tall, cold glass from her hand and following her into the living room. Some things change, and some don't, I observed as I plopped down next to her on the brown sectional. Whatever was going on, Annemarie still liked to take charge of a situation. "So," I said. "Do I need to return my dress?"

"Harsh, as always," said Annemarie. She cocked her head to the side and looked at me quizzically. "But something's different."

"Oh?" For some inexplicable reason, I felt my cheeks color.

"Yeah," said Annemarie with a grin. "You're glowing. Something's making you happy."

I took a swig of icy, sour-sweet lemonade, and once again thanked my grandma for teaching me how to make it. "Mmmm," I mumbled.

"That good?" said Annemarie. "Come on, fess up."

"That was about the lemonade," I said, gently slapping her bare knee. "Are you avoiding my question?"

"No," she said. "And no."

"Sorry, I don't speak in code. Explain, please."

"No, I'm not avoiding your question, and no you don't have to sell your dress."

I put my glass on the coffee table. "You're still getting married?" Annemarie nodded, and the flood of relief I felt surprised me. "Thank god," I said, taking her hands in mine. "Are you going to tell me what happened?"

"Eventually," she said. "But for now, suffice it to say that Richard and I are okay."

"So where did you go this weekend?"

"To a friend's cottage."

I detected a mischief in her voice that could only mean one thing. "What kind of friend?"

"A good one," she said, her eyes twinkling. Trying to get my brain around her and Jenn and Iona was hard enough. Was I to about to find out she'd gone off with someone else, too?

"Annemarie," I said. "What the fuck is going on?"

She smiled at me. "I'm evolving," she said. "Richard and I are evolving."

"You mean, you're fucking other people?"

Annemarie looked surprised. "Why would you think that?"

"Give it up, Annemarie," I said. "I know all about Jenn and Iona."

"Kissing and telling," said Annemarie. "That's low."

"Not really," I said. "Jenn and I tell each other everything."

Annemarie raised an eyebrow. "Like us?"

"Once upon a time, maybe," I said. "Not lately, apparently."

Annemarie moved closer to me on the couch. "I'm sorry," she said. "Things have been hard."

I nodded, feeling tears well up. "I still can't believe you fucked Jenn and Iona."

"Geez, Lilah," said Annemarie. "You make it sound like a huge thing. You've been polyamorous since I've known you. I thought you'd be thrilled."

"I might be," I said. "Eventually. Right now I'm just shocked."

Annemarie looked me square in the eye. "And why should you be so shocked? You've known for a long time what's been on Richard's mind."

I met her gaze without flinching. "True," I said. "That's true."

"Why didn't you talk to me?"

"It wasn't my place. And it's not like Richard actually told me. At least not until last week, at which point I told him he had to talk to you." Annemarie was still looking at me squarely, and I realized my heart was pounding. "Annemarie. You don't think–" There was no need to finish the sentence.

"No," she said. "I know nothing happened between you two. But not because you didn't want it to."

Heat rushed into my cheeks, fueled by embarrassment. "Annemarie," I protested. "I love you."

She took my hands. "I know you do," she said. "I'm not accusing you of anything, except not talking to me, and I probably bear some responsibility for that, too."

"Why didn't you tell me about Jenn?" I asked.

"I was busy trying to figure things out," she said.

"Without me," I said, surprised at the bitterness in my voice.

"Now, now," said Annemarie. "Jealousy doesn't become you."

"Sorry," I said. "You're changing so much; it's scaring me."

Annemarie put two fingers under my chin and pulled me closer to her. "I love you as much as ever," she said. "And it's not like you've told me what's going on with you. Something, obviously." The reminder of Chad sent a thrill through me, which Annemarie somehow felt, too. "Whoa, girl. What's up?"

How to say everything that was going on inside me? How to put it into words? I settled for just one. "Chad," I whispered.

"Chad? That floppy-haired kitchen helper?"

"Don't look so surprised," I said.

"I didn't imagine he was your type," said Annemarie, laughing.

"Why not?" I asked indignantly.

"I don't know," she said. "Too–straight?"

"Honestly, Annemarie," I said. "Didn't anyone ever tell you not to judge a book by its cover? You don't know the first thing about him."

"You're right," she said. "So tell me. What's the first thing?"

Once again, there was just too much to say about Chad's good qualities. So I settled for expressing my fears. "He's not bi, and he's not poly."

"That's two things."

"Oh, shut up," I said, giving her a smack on the thigh. "This is serious."

"So," she said, with what seemed like amusement. "Now you're the one with the problem."

"Not really a problem," I said. "Not yet."

Annemarie looked skeptical. "How so?"

"Not a problem because," I said, shrugging, "I don't want to fuck anyone else?" I said it like a question because I still wasn't sure whether it really wasn't a problem, or whether it was a really big problem.

"Well, whaddaya know." Annemarie said it like she'd just uncovered the eighth wonder of the world.

"What's that supposed to mean?"

"You must be in love." She slapped me on the back and laughed. "I never thought I'd see the day," she said.

I wasn't sure whether Annemarie was right, but I didn't bother trying to deny it. I had bigger worries. "I can't fall in love like some normal person," I said. "I'm a bisexual, polyamorous woman. I can't do that."

"So what," said Annemarie.

"That's disrespectful," I said. "I know you've never approved of my lifestyle, but that's really shitty, not to mention hypocritical."

Annemarie screwed her face into a sneer. "Hypocritical?"

"You and Richard have some kind of god knows what arrangement, and you're so whatting my choices?"

"No," she said. "Not at all. I'm just saying, who needs the labels?"

"I do," I said.

"Why?" she asked.

"Because they're who I am."

Annemarie shook her head. "No," she said. "Lilah is who you are."

"I worked hard to figure out those labels," I said. "It wasn't easy."

"I know," said Annemarie. "But are they helping you figure this out?"

"No," I agreed. We sat quietly for a minute, Annemarie sipping her lemonade, me sucking on what was left of my ice cubes. I voiced my current greatest fears. "What if it comes back?" I whispered, swallowing a half-melted chunk of ice. "And what if it doesn't?"

"You're the one who meditates," said Annemarie. "You ought to know the answer to that."

Indeed I did. I closed my eyes and took a deep breath, and let the fear have its way with me, and remembered what Chad said.

*We'll figure it out.*

I snuggled up to Annemarie. "I love you," I said.

"Me, too," she answered, pushing me gently away. "Now get me some more lemonade, and when you get back, you better be ready to talk."

I took her glass and mine, and filled them to the brim.

## EPILOGUE

"You feel so good, baby."

Richard's hands cradled Annemarie's perfect, lube-covered breasts, using them to smother his cock. Her hands were tied to their marriage bed with the veil that had been on her head just hours before, when they'd said their vows in front of a full congregation of friends and family.

Their parents had been there, looking pleased and proud, and Lilah, too, looking hotter than ever in the gown Annemarie had chosen for her, flanked by her boyfriend who clearly had it bad for her, and judging by the way she looked at him, it went both ways, which was kind of shocking, but since the day he and Annemarie had nixed their crisis and cemented their wedding plans for good and all, Richard had learned not to be surprised by much of anything when it came to matters of the heart, or matters of the flesh.

Who would have thought, for example, that Zachary Link, Annemarie's lover, and now a mentor of sorts to the both of them, would attend their wedding with his wife? Or that Jenn and her butch, Iona, who had shown both Annemarie and Richard a good time, separately and together, in all combinations, would be beaming so proudly as they walked down the aisle?

None of his colleagues from the office would have any idea, certainly, about the deep and thrilling relationship he enjoyed with this woman he loved so dearly.

"Richard." Annemarie moaned as he slid his cock in and out of the slick passageway between her breasts. She lowered her head, trying to take the head of his cock into her mouth. He teased her, nudging her chin with it, even rubbing her lips with it before taking it away and burying it again in the hot chasm of her breasts. "Give me," she pleaded. "I want it."

Richard scooched forward until he was kneeling over her face, his balls dangling on her chin and his erect cock directly over her mouth. "At your service, Mrs. Samson."

Annemarie licked him with her tongue, trying to maneuver him into her mouth. He helped out and guided his cock there, letting her suck appreciatively for a few minutes, enjoying the feel, so wet, so warm, and so urgent. Then he turned his body and leaned over so he could take her into his mouth, too, licking until she came, holding her ass cheeks as she did, feeling them contract and tighten in his hands.

"Now I want to fuck my wife," he said, turning around and kissing her deeply.

They looked into each other's eyes for a moment, smiling. "I love you, Richard," she said. "My Richard."

"I love you, too, my Annemarie," he answered, ripping the veils into shreds to release her hands. She grabbed onto him, hugging him tightly, then he turned her over and took her from behind, nice and slow, just the way she liked it, until he felt the wave build and crest, and he sped up, faster and faster, fucking Annemarie all the way home.

If you enjoyed this story, you can sign up for a free membership at ForbiddenFiction and discuss it with other readers and the author at the *You Complicate Me* story page.

We do our best to proof all our work, but if you spot a text error we missed, please let us know via our website Contact Form.

# Author's Notes

We've all heard the statistics — marriage in the modern world ain't easy or simple. Despite that, or perhaps because of it, a happy marriage is often considered the relationship holy grail. Books, articles, products, and therapists that help people enhance, enliven, or even rescue their long term relationships are everywhere.

As I've observed my friends and acquaintances take the marriage leap, it's become clear to me that happily ever after can look radically different than the boy meets girl fairy tales that have been shoved down our throats for so long. Of course, sex isn't often prominent in those stories. It's simply an unquestionable given that the straight, monogamous couples involved in them are being fulfilled in every way possible.

What happens to the people who aren't in those stories? What does it mean for them to commit to a relationship or marriage? What does it mean to be a friend? How do they become their best selves? These are some of the questions I explored while writing "At Your Service." I was interested in the ways people who love sex and want to have it with multiple partners navigate their relationships and desires.

Annemarie's repression works for a long time, but her fiancée (is it any accident she fell for someone who's also a closeted poly person?) forces her to take a long, hard look at what she really wants. Lilah takes the opposite tack and zealously pursues multiple lovers, but in the process she misses the heady experience of falling in love. When she does, she understands the appeal of monogamy (at least for the moment).

Getting inside their heads and their sex lives proved to be great fun. I love writing sex scenes, but two of my favorites were Lilah's first romp with Jenn and Iona, and the sex den that Lilah finds herself in after the Eats concert. I also enjoyed creating the scene when Richard literally ties Annemarie's hands, and she ambivalently but ecstatically cedes her position as the bedroom top.

Another important directive for me was to portray strong, independent women who are in charge of their bodies and their destinies. Lilah and Annemarie have their challenges, but they handle the bumps in their roads with courage and fierceness. They know that complexity, while sometimes creating confusion, also offers unimagined options and opportunities for freedom.

My thanks to G.D. — my life partner and supporter of all my endeavors. Thanks and accolades also go to Anna Watson, fellow erotica writer and dear friend.

# About the Author

**Alicia Wag** resides in Massachusetts and is the author of *Mrs. M.: A Book of Erotic Stories*. Her work has been published in *Just Watch Me: Erotica for Women*, *The Mammoth Book of Best New Erotica 2007*, *Sixteen of the Best (Sara Veitch Spanking Stories)*, Clean Sheets, Penthouse Variations, and other publications. Besides writing juicy stories, she enjoys singing, cooking, movies, and good conversation.

# About the Publisher

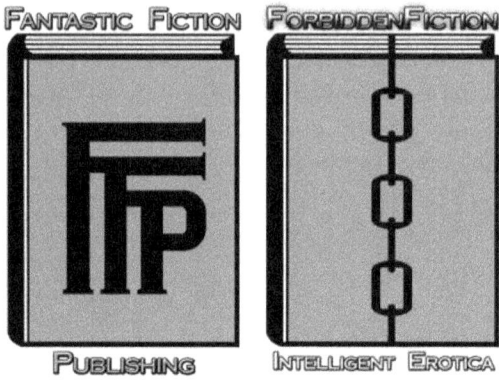

**ForbiddenFiction.com** is a publisher devoted to writing that breaks the boundaries of original erotic fiction. Our stories combine intense sexuality with quality writing. Stories at Forbidden Fiction.com not only arouse readers through sensations, but also engage them emotionally and mentally through storytelling as well-crafted as the sex is hot.

ForbiddenFiction.com is also designed to be a social reading environment. You'll have fun even if just reading the latest post each day, yet you will have the chance for so much more. Readers and authors can be part of ongoing discussions of specific works and individual authors as well as more general topics.

Sign up for a FREE Membership today at ForbiddenFiction.com